the breakfast club

Nat's Bridesmaid Blues

Kate Costelloe

Hodder
Children's
Books

A division of Hachette Children's Books

ISBN-13: 978 1 444 90286 0

Typeset in AGaramond by Avon DataSet Ltd,
Bidford on Avon, Warwickshire

Printed and bound by CPI Group (UK) Ltd,
Croydon, CR0 4YY

The paper and board used in this paperback by Hodder Children's Books
are natural recyclable products made from wood grown in
sustainable forests. The manufacturing processes conform to the
environmental regulations of the country of origin.

Hodder Children's Books
a division of Hachette Children's Books
338 Euston Road, London NW1 3BH
An Hachette Livre UK Company

For Dre, with love and thanks

Chapter One

It was Saturday morning and just starting to get light. Everyone else in our house was asleep as I tiptoed down from my attic room.

I'd showered, washed and dried my hair and got dressed as far as my unsexy white Marks and Sparks underwear. With my latest vintage find over my arm, I was stealthily heading for my sister Plum's room on the first floor.

Plum was staying over at her boyfriend's, something she did pretty often these days. Dad and my stepmother were sleeping off the effects of a boozy dinner with some of Dad's work colleagues, and my sister Nelly likes to sleep late at weekends. It was unlikely I'd be disturbed.

Yet as I padded down the silent corridors, I felt uncomfortably exposed, as if I was being filmed by a hidden CCTV camera. I was on an extremely private and personal mission, the kind that only another insecure fourteen-year-old girl in need of a full-length mirror could understand. In a few hours I was meeting the other girls in the Breakfast Club. Today was a major red letter day for everyone and I wanted to look my best.

I was tiptoeing extra carefully now, in case I set off the creaky floorboard outside Nellie's room. Nellie's full name is Eleanor but everyone still uses her hideous baby-name, even Rupert, her long-term boyfriend.

Unfortunately for me Nellie didn't spend nearly as much time with Rupert as Plum spent with Gus. When my sisters were at home, they tended to gang up with my stepmum; constant little nitpicks about my looks or the sloppy way I stand or how many pieces of toast I stuffed down at breakfast. The slightest thing could set them off. That's why I'd got up at dawn to sneak an illicit peep in my sister's mirror so I could avoid any snide comments.

Plum's room is now so different to the rest of our house that I got an actual physical jolt every time I crossed the threshold. When she was ten years old she stuck a notice on her door: *Bratty Little Sisters KEEP OUT (that means YOU Natalie!)* and her room still felt like forbidden ground as I softly turned the door handle and crept in.

Sometimes I hear girls talk about their older sisters; how they borrow their clothes and help them get ready for parties, and I feel as if I must have grown up on a different planet. My sisters never went to parties, or if they did they kept it a deadly secret. When they eventually hit their teens they didn't start slapping on too much make-up or get piercings. They did something far more shocking. They turned into younger versions of Jenny.

Jenny did her hair in a French pleat like it was the 1950s and so did they. Jenny bought her skirts from Country Casuals and so did they. Jenny could tell you how many calories there are in a single slice of cucumber and so could they. Dieting became their second favourite shared topic for discussion (their first favourite topic being me). Then Plum met Gus and almost overnight she changed. She dumped the Country Casuals, started buying super-sleek outfits from all Gus's favourite designers, and redecorated her room in the pale neutrals Gus prefers; Ella calls them 'non-colours'. You won't see any of that old style clutter in Plum's room that you see in the rest of our house. Everything is totally subtle, tasteful and new.

Despite hardly ever being at home Plum still kept her queen-sized bed immaculately made up, with cushions and throws like a bed in one of those chic boutique hotels. The room smelled of her favourite green tea perfume. (It was Gus's favourite so now obviously it was hers.) Beside her bed was a chunky scented candle (green tea and fig), and a framed photo of Plum and Gus looking all loved-up on a recent scuba-diving holiday.

I think my sisters are really pretty. Lately Nellie has taken to wearing younger and more stylish clothes like Plum and they both have this long honey-coloured perfectly glossy hair. My friends say my sisters are too skinny, but I doubt if either Plum or Nelly would understand the concept of 'too skinny'. My stepmum definitely wouldn't.

Plum's no-colour cotton rug felt firm and nubbly under my bare feet as I stole over to the window and carefully raised the blinds to halfway. Like a searchlight, the early morning light went streaming directly on to Plum's mirror. I quickly averted my eyes and went to sit on my sister's bed, rubbing the gooseflesh on my arms.

The Breakfast Club's unwritten rule is that everybody turns up in the clothes they feel happiest in.

My friends would be appalled if they knew I was working myself into a complete froth over a stupid outfit. I *did* get that it was dumb. I was just desperate to look as pretty as the others. I was scared of letting myself – or them – down.

I ran into Ella and Billie on my very first day at my new school. I say I ran into them, but it's more like they rugby tackled me in the playground! I had left my boarding school under a bit of a cloud – actually a lot of a cloud. Ella says they took one look at me tottering in through our school gates on my jelly legs and decided I needed rescuing. Then after we'd known each other a while they started saying that they must introduce me to Lexie Brown.

Lexie, Ella and Billie all used to attend the same Notting Hill primary school. The three of them were completely inseparable, staying at each other's houses, borrowing each other's hair-brushes and clothes. Then Lexie's family moved to Shepherd's Bush and it probably seemed like that was the end of the notorious gang of three. That is unless you know Lexie, Ella and Billie! They'd never ever lost touch, emailing and texting when they couldn't meet up.

When I eventually met this mysterious Lexie I'd heard so much about who called her mum and dad by their first names and learned to ice skate almost as soon as she could walk, it was by accident. I was just coming up out of the Underground at Notting Hill when I bumped into my new friends, who were enthusiastically thumping a third girl on the back, trying to cure her of a dramatic choking fit. I quickly took in her charcoal-grey hoodie and the skinny jeans worn with soft Ugg boots with the fleecy tops turned down and realised that this had to be the legendary Lexie. It turned out she had drained the last of her Pepsi a bit too enthusiastically and it had gone down the wrong way. My first glimpse of Lexie was this spluttering wreck with brown bubbles coming down her nose!

Once Lexie had recovered her breath and her dignity, Billie quickly made the introductions and luckily Lexie and I clicked. I say 'luckily', because if she hadn't liked me she'd have made it crystal clear. Lexie is the kind of girl who believes in speaking her mind.

'Were you actually *born* in this house?' she asked with a shiver the first time I'd invited them back for tea. I just nodded and she said sympathetically, 'Wow, it must be like growing up inside a museum!'

I didn't know what to say, so I quipped, 'Yeah, a museum where they let dogs chew the exhibits!'

(My stepmother breeds cocker spaniels.) It was only later that I realised it wasn't just the portraits of my ancestors in their Tudor ruffs or the looming heirloom furniture that my new friends found off-putting. It was my actual *family* – mostly my stepmother and sisters.

'Is your stepmum always that patronising?' Lexie had demanded, with her usual bluntness after that same visit.

'Did you think she was patronising?' I asked in surprise. It had never occurred to me to judge Jenny's behaviour. In our family it's my stepmother who does the judging.

'She's a bit *more* than patronising!' Billie had said with feeling. 'She looks total daggers at us like we're going to nick the family silver and sell it for Class A drugs! Your dad is a sweetie though,' she'd added quickly, obviously feeling she'd been a bit harsh.

'He's more like Nat! She's a sweetie too!' Ella had agreed, hugging me, and I felt this amazed relief flood through me. Despite the chilly reception they'd had from Jenny and my sisters, Ella and the others wanted to be my friends! I can't tell you what a huge moment this was. For as long as I could remember I'd been told that I was a Bonneville-St John, distantly related to the royal family, and that I must live up to my name. I'd grown up believing that my family was the most important thing about me. But my new friends didn't give two hoots about my connection with William and Harry. They just cared about me!

I'd known the others for almost six months when we reinvented ourselves as the Breakfast Club. We were at Lexie's house and it was raining and Ella was in a bad mood because she had just had a big fight with her mum. The new horror DVD we'd been looking forward to all week had turned out to be about as exciting as cBeebies. The DVD was the last straw for Ella and she went into this long rant. She said it totally sucked being fourteen. She was sick of hanging around just watching lame DVDs and playing Xbox. She didn't want to have to spend her teens on hold waiting; waiting to grow up, waiting so we could do real life things like get flats and jobs and stay out clubbing till late, then go out for breakfast in some quirky café.

That's when Ella had the revelation that changed our lives. 'OMG!' she gasped. 'We might be too young to get jobs and too hard-up to rent our own flat, but nobody could object to us going out to a cool café for breakfast.'

It's the kind of genius idea that seems so obvious

once someone else has said it out loud. In a weird way it felt like something that was actually *waiting* to happen. It would be like a tiny taste of independence, a chance to get away by ourselves without parents or annoying siblings breathing down our necks. But the Breakfast Club is about much more than that. It's not just girls gossiping and sharing their problems, though we do that too. It's about being the best selves we know how to be, making plans, dreaming dreams; what Ella calls being our 'superstar celebrity selves'.

Since that rainy spring day we haven't looked back! I don't think it's an exaggeration to say that Saturday mornings at Mario's are the thing we most look forward to all week. Ella says being in the Breakfast Club is better than therapy. I tell her I'll take her word for that; I think my family would sooner send me to a voodoo priestess than let me have therapy.

Anyway, today was an extra-special day for us Breakfast Clubbers. For two heart-stopping weeks we thought we'd lost our special café for ever after the landlord decided to sell it to a property developer. Mario's is special to all of us but it had super-special associations for me because we found it on the same day that I first met Lexie and was officially accepted into their little group. Ella is a great one for signs and omens and she says the fact that we found our perfect café on the same day that all four of us officially became friends was a Sign that the Breakfast Club was meant to be.

Then, less than six months after we'd found it, our perfect café got cruelly whisked away and we were all totally gutted. Luckily, this story had a surprise fairytale ending. Totally unexpectedly, Mario inherited a fortune from his elderly aunt and was able to buy the café premises outright.

When we heard the news we literally danced in the street. That's how much we all adore Mario's! My friends say it's like a home from home and I always agree, even though Mario's is nothing like my home. It's cosy and friendly, also you get mouth-wateringly delicious food.

In my house, there's one shelf in our huge old relic of a fridge that is always kept full and that's for my dad to graze on when he gets back from the City. My stepmother fills the remaining shelves with low-calorie ready meals, and tonic water and nets of lemons. It's not surprising that I spend my week thinking longingly about what I'm going to order at Mario's.

Just thinking about it now set my tummy off in a long ferocious gurgle. I took a deep breath. *Get on with it, Natalie*, I thought, *unless you're planning to go out to breakfast in your bra and knickers?*

Bravely positioning myself in front of Plum's three-way mirror, I slipped the silky tea dress over my head and after a short struggle succeeded in zipping it up. The 1950s dress was the total opposite of no-coloured. It was flaming scarlet with a splashy retro print. Ella had spotted it on a vintage stall the previous week and made me try it on right then and there. My friends had all taken turns to peer into my cramped little changing booth so they could give me their verdicts.

Ella was first. 'Oh my God! Move *over*, Gok Wan!' Then she turned around and boasted to the others, 'I am *such* a talented stylist. That fitted fifties style is perfect on her!'

Then Billie had poked her head in. 'You look *gorgeous*, girl,' she'd agreed, nodding. 'If I looked that good in dresses I'd never wear jeans again!' Lexie said enviously. I had looked at myself in the smeary little mirror and I had smiled the *biggest* smile. It was like I was seeing myself through their eyes and I really *did* look gorgeous!

But the minute I'd brought my vintage purchase back home, the doubts started crowding in. They were crowding in now as I anxiously twisted and turned in front of the mirror.

The dress was designed to be clingy, but was it *too* clingy? I tried sucking in my breath to reduce the cling factor, but that just made my boobs stick out like tiny torpedoes. I could already hear Jenny's huff of disgust. 'Well, *that* doesn't leave much to the imagination, Natalie!' She was always telling me to cover myself up or 'people' (i.e. boys) would get 'the wrong idea'.

I shut my eyes and imagined that my friends were here to support me. I knew exactly what Billie would say, 'Don't listen to those three stick insects, girl! Curvy and happy is the way forward!'

Lexie would say something like, 'Feel pretty and you'll *be* pretty.' And Ella would say, 'Natalie, sometimes you've got to fake it until you make it!'

I followed their advice. I smiled flirtatiously at my reflection, then I did the same flirty smile but this time bashfully looking up under my lashes at my (purely imaginary) boyfriend. I lifted up a handful of brown curls, pouting in what I hoped was a sexy manner, but my reflection looked as if it was about to burst into tears. I let the hank of hair fall back in despair. My new dress was a disaster. Correction; the dress was every bit as gorgeous as my friends had said. It was the girl inside who was a disaster. I wanted to be sexy and sassy, I just didn't know how.

Unlike me, my friends always seemed to know exactly who they are. Ella is the Breakfast Club's Boho princess. Outside school, she dresses in gypsy skirts, lacy tops and her favourite pair of lilac Doc Martens. Billie is effortlessly street in checked shirts and denim. Sporty Lexie goes for hoodies, T-shirts and skinny jeans. *How come they just know who to be?* I asked myself in despair.

I'd asked Ella that question once and she just said, 'Who do you *want* to be?' I'd said, 'I have NO idea,' and burst into tears.

I was almost in tears now. I crumpled on to my sister's bed, hugging one of her no-coloured cushions to my chest. Why couldn't I be *normal* like everyone else? OK, so it didn't help being called Natalie Cordelia Bonneville-St John. Not exactly a name to make you blend into the crowd. It also didn't help that I'm three inches taller than most girls my age, or that I sound a tiny bit posh.

Everyone in my family sounds posh, the same as everyone in my family gets sent off to boarding school as soon as they can tie their own laces. I'd been a boarder since I was eight years old. I'd actually loved it at St Winifred's, my prep school. It was small and homey and I made some good friends. Then, when it was time to move up into the seniors, my stepmother got it into her head that I wasn't being sufficiently 'stretched' so I was moved to a well-known girls' school on the Sussex coast where my stepmother had once been a star hockey player.

My first report said I was 'bright but not brilliant'. It wasn't enough to be just 'bright' at that school. You had to be 'brilliant' or everybody thought that you were just a waste of space. I might have tried harder to shine but it was taking most of my energy not to be noticed. I specifically didn't want to be noticed by Olivia and Georgia McVeigh. I don't know why people are so surprised to learn that posh schools have bullies. I managed to keep under the McVeigh twins' radar for almost two years but I always knew that one day it would be my turn and one day it was.

Those girls should actually write a handbook on bullying because they knew every spiteful trick going; leaving malicious messages pinned to my pillow for me to find before I went to sleep, circulating hideous untrue rumours. Even my one or two small successes they found a way to poison. They were evil but they were brilliantly cunningly evil and I don't think our teachers ever had an inkling what was going on – and obviously I never told because we Bonneville-St Johns never tell tales.

After a few months of the McVeigh treatment, I started having some weird symptoms. I'd be sitting in class and I'd suddenly be unable to breathe and almost black out. I didn't know what was happening to me. I thought, (actually I kind of *hoped*) that I might be dying.

The matron took me to the doctor, who talked to me for ages and then diagnosed panic attacks. It was the first time I'd heard of them since it goes without saying that the Bonneville-St Johns never get panic attacks. The doctor said my stress levels were sky high and wondered aloud if my school might not be the right one for me.

My stepmother said this was all nonsense. I was just going through a bit of a rough patch and it would pass. I wasn't and it didn't. I panicked all day and cried myself to sleep all night. There was only one girl who was in worse shape than me and that was Sarah Corrie and she had major anorexia. Then one day her parents took her away and that just left me, silently weeping into my lumpy school pillow.

I wrote pleading with my parents to let me come home (I couldn't phone in case someone overheard and reported back to the twins) but since I couldn't tell them about the bullying, I didn't seriously believe anyone would take any notice. But someone did.

For the first time, my dad went against Jenny's wishes, driving down to Sussex and calmly packing me and my belongings inside his gleaming silver Saab. I watched that ivy-covered hellhole disappearing for ever in the rear-view mirror and shakily wondered if this was all just a wonderful dream.

I thought my dad would drive me straight home in disgusted silence. Instead he drove us to a nearby steak house and ordered us both steak and chips with all the trimmings.

'I'm so sorry,' I told him when I had gobbled down every delicious mouthful. 'I tried to make it work. I really did.'

He set down his knife and fork and I braced myself to be told what a disappointment I was. 'I blame myself,' he said gruffly to my astonishment. 'I never thought it was the right school for you. I shouldn't have let myself be talked round. You're like your mother; sensitive.' Then he beckoned our waitress over and asked for a jug of tap water while I sat fighting back tears of happiness and relief.

I could count on the fingers of one hand the number

of times I'd heard my mother mentioned by a member of my family. I sometimes felt like I wasn't even supposed to *think* about her. Now not only had my dad told me I was like her, he made it sound as if being sensitive was actually a good quality and not a fatal flaw as my stepmother seemed to think.

While we ate our painfully too-hot apple pie with painfully cold vanilla ice cream (Dad joked that we might get electric shocks), he explained that Jenny had already lined up several private day-schools for me to visit. Still glowing from my dad's words, I had a rare burst of courage. 'Dad, I'd rather go to a normal London school if that's all right.'

His eyebrows went up like two woolly grey caterpillars. 'A *state* school? Jenny won't like that, and I'm not sure you will either.' But I just repeated that it's what I wanted and he reluctantly agreed to give it a try.

I'd been away from my home for almost two months. For most of that time I'd been an emotional wreck. I'd also been wearing my hideous school uniform seven days a week. Possibly that's why I'd never noticed that despite being too unhappy to eat most days, I had somehow developed curves where I had previously just been straight up and down.

My stepmum noticed though. She noticed the minute I climbed out of the car. She gave me one withering head-to-toe glance that made me want to crawl into the nearest hole and die. 'Oh, *dear*, Natalie,' she drawled. 'What *are* we going to do about all that excess *weight*?'

After that she monitored everything that passed my lips, counting up my daily calorie intake and telling me when I was over my daily limit. On my first day at my new school, Billie took one look at the rice cakes Jenny had given me for my packed lunch and she dumped them in the bin! Billie said rice cakes were polystyrene tiles sold under another name and anybody with half a brain knew that eating polystyrene was wrong!

I let out a surprise snicker of laughter at the memory. Remembering how Billie and Ella had befriended me suddenly made me feel better. *Count your blessings, Natalie*, I thought. *You could still be at that boarding school being persecuted by the evil McVeigh twins.*

Thanks to my dad, not only had I got away, I'd found real friends to support me. Why was I obsessing about my looks! I was going to be with my BFFs and they thought I was gorgeous no matter what!

I uncurled myself from my sister's bed and beamed at my reflection in the mirror, a proper smile this time.

The smile lit up my face, and at that moment, from that particular angle, I thought I looked almost pretty. I would wear the red tea dress after all. I would be the vintage-wearing friend, the curvy, unconfident one who was still trying to figure out who she wanted to be.

I was startled by the scrape of a key turning in the lock, followed by a brisk electric beep as someone switched off the burglar alarm. Next minute my sister Plum came rushing up the stairs. 'Everybody, wake up! I've got some news!' Her voice was sharp with excitement.

Without thinking I ran to the door. 'Oh my God, what happened?'

Instead of demanding what I was doing in her room, or what I thought I looked like in that ridiculous dress, my sister threw her arms around me. 'Gus proposed! He's just stopped off to buy some champagne! I'm getting married!' She was almost crying with happiness. 'Oh, Nat, I'm going to have *such* a beautiful wedding, and you're going to be a *bridesmaid,* isn't that thrilling!'

I'd been mercifully free of panic attacks since the day I left my boarding school but for a terrible moment I thought they'd come back. My vision blurred and my heart pounded like a drum. I had this spine-chilling picture of myself looking like that beefy girl in Muriel's

Wedding, except I was the beefy bridesmaid obviously, not the bride; a kind of nightmare Bridesmaidzilla.

I pictured myself galumphing down the aisle behind Plum and Gus, wearing a lopsided floral crown and trying not to trip on the hem of my dress (or even worse, go pinging across the church in those scary magic knickers Jenny makes me wear to family functions), and I pictured my stepmother watching with narrow-eyed disapproval every step of the way.

My terror must have shown on my face because Plum immediately pulled me into her room, and dropped her voice to a whisper. 'You don't need to worry about a thing, sweetie. Don't worry about letting me down, because you won't, and don't worry about Jenny because you are going to be *the* most exquisite bridesmaid ever!'

At that moment, all my fears melted away and I felt a huge rush of love for my sister; my real sister, the one who let me crawl into her bed when I'd had a bad dream. I had always loved her underneath. I'd just learned that it wasn't very smart to let it show. Plum was saying I didn't have to worry. She *trusted* me to be a beautiful bridesmaid. I'd never heard her use the word 'exquisite' about anyone before, let alone her ugly duckling youngest sister.

All the same I was puzzled. 'Why don't I have to worry about Jenny?'

'Because Gus and I have got it all handled,' Plum said briskly.

I giggled. She made it sound like they were planning to have my stepmother kidnapped! I adored this new conspiratorial Plum and for a moment I think she adored me. We beamed shyly at each other as I waited for her to explain.

'Gus has offered to hire us a personal trainer to get us all into shape for our wedding. Jacek absolutely guarantees he can get us to drop two dress sizes in two months! We are all going to look like supermodels, Natalie! Well, *say* something!'

'I – I'm speechless,' I said, which was God's honest truth. 'I'm just SO totally speechless!' And because I wanted to hang on to this strangely loveable big sister for a moment longer, I gave her a shy hug and said dutifully, 'Congratulations, I hope you and Gus will be really happy.'

Then the doorbell rang and Plum said, 'That'll be Gus, with the champagne. Natkins, run down and let him in, will you? I'll go and wake up all these sleepyheads so we can tell them our news.'

As I opened the door to my future brother-in-law,

two thoughts flashed simultaneously across my mind. I wondered if Gus, who I noticed was developing a serious belly, would be hiring a trainer to get *him* into shape for his big day? I also thought that I'd better order a stonkingly *huge* breakfast at Mario's, because it was going to be the last decent meal I'd get until after the wedding.

Chapter Two

We called ourselves the Breakfast Club because it was the obvious name, also because we just *lurved* that old 80s movie with Judd Nelson playing the sexy bad boy from the wrong side of the tracks. We don't have actual rules (like Lexie says, we're not five) but we do have one or two little traditions. For instance my friends understand that, after a week of low-calorie diet food, I can't hear a word anybody says until I've had at least a few mouthfuls of something to eat. So we try to save any real earth-shaking news until a good fifteen minutes into breakfast.

This morning, though, *I* was the girl with the earth-shaking news. I was also shockingly late. I'm one of those super-eager people, embarrassingly early for everything. But thanks to our early morning wedding excitement I'd got seriously held up. When I eventually walked in, Mario gave me a huge grin. 'Natalie, *cara*! It's good to see you again.'

I shyly said something about it being good to see them too, but I was secretly checking around, worried in case the newly refurbished Mario's turned out to be a disappointment. It wasn't. It just looked like a subtly upgraded version of the Mario's we all knew and loved. Everything was comfortingly familiar: cosy private booths, framed photographs of Mario's regulars, including local celebs like Lily Allen. Even the smell was the same, I thought, as I inhaled the blissful aroma of roasted coffee beans, rich Italian chocolate, cinnamon and vanilla that is Mario's signature scent.

I saw Lexie crane around the corner of our favourite booth. She must have heard my voice, 'Yay, *finally*!' she cheered. 'We were just going to send out a search party!'

'We got you a cappuccino!' called Ella from inside the booth.

I wriggled out of my jacket and went to slide in beside Billie. As usual she looked amazing in one of those street little tops she always manages to find. The olive green checks totally set off her cinnamon-coloured skin and glossy dark curls. 'You look good, girl!' she said approvingly.

I felt my cheeks going hot. 'You all look great too,' I said, embarrassed.

Ella looked typically like she'd stepped out of a *Company* magazine photo shoot in her loose white shirt, with a skimpy little nut-brown velvet skirt over leggings, topped with a grey trilby hat! Ella is the Breakfast Club's very own fashionista. When she leaves school she wants to study fashion design at St Martin's.

Lexie was wearing a typical Lexie outfit: skinny jeans, pristine new trainers and a white T-shirt that said in teeny-tiny writing, '*If you can read this you're standing WAY too close!*' Lexie has generally put in two hours' practice at the ice rink by the time she meets us at Mario's, which was possibly why she looked so pale. What with ice skating, school work and helping out with her little brothers, Lexie doesn't get much downtime and for the first time I thought it was starting to show.

'Ahem,' said a familiar husky voice. Mario's daughter Jools was standing ready with her notepad. 'Are you all ready to order now Natalie's here?'

Jools is only a few years older than us. As usual she wore her trademark silver earrings, five or six on each ear, and a couple more in her nose. We'd met Jools for the first time on the same day we discovered Hillgate

Place and Mario's. She seems to genuinely like all of us, but she and Billie have become firm friends, partly through their shared interest in music. As well as being a normal café Mario's has a bar where they sometimes play live music. Jools was talking about letting Billie do an early DJ slot even before the café was threatened with closure. But after Billie performed her own songs at a fundraiser Jools organised for her friend's little girl, Jools became even more determined to showcase this budding young artist who was also a real Notting Hill girl.

When Jools had gone off with our order, Billie gave me one of her searching looks. 'Are you OK, Natz?' she asked.

I'd been going to wait fifteen minutes. I swear I'd been going to wait, but the genuine concern in Billie's eyes tipped me over the edge. 'I am SO not OK!' I said dramatically. 'My sister Plum is getting married!'

I was expecting gasps of sympathy but Ella just looked vague. 'Which boyfriend is Plum's one again, Ben or Jerry?' My friends always claim they can't remember my sister's boyfriend's names, and I have to say Gus and Rupert are very similar City types.

'Nellie is dating Rupert,' I explained for the umpteenth time. 'Gus proposed to Plum last night

26

and they're having a huge wedd—'

'Oh my GOD!' Ella gasped, beating me to it. 'She wants you to be her *BRIDESMAID*!'

'I've been a bridesmaid a few times,' Lexie said airily. 'It's not *that* bad.'

'It *is* that bad', I said miserably. 'Plum wants to turn us all into supermodels for her big day so she's persuaded Gus to hire us a personal trainer.'

A stunned silence followed my announcement.

At last Billie said, 'A personal trainer for *all* of you?' I just nodded and she gave a low whistle. 'He must be RICH!'

'He is, and Plum says this trainer absolutely guarantees to make us drop two dress sizes in two months.'

'*Two* months to be a supermodel! She doesn't want much!' Ella said.

'Is that even *legal*?' Lexie asked, amazed.

'If Plum drops another two dress sizes she'll disappear completely,' Billie scoffed.

Lexie was trying to figure something out. 'Are you saying Gus or whatever his name is only proposed last night and they're planning to get married in *two* months? I thought people usually give themselves like a year to organise things?'

My dad had said something similar. He'd taken Gus out into the garden, asking him straight out if there was any particular reason for their hurry. I wasn't supposed to hear, but I was in the kitchen sneaking an emergency piece of toast and the window was open.

Gus was very polite and correct. He said there was indeed a particular reason, but not the one my dad was hinting at. Gus had been headhunted for a top banking job in Singapore. The contract was for three years, and he'd decided he couldn't honourably ask Plum to come with him unless they were married, plus he'd decided it would be much easier for all their friends and relatives if the wedding was in the UK. I relayed this piece of news to my friends.

'Singapore, wow!' said Billie. 'Your sister will be able to travel to so many amazing places from there. Thailand, Hong Kong, Japan . . .'

'Imagine the *fabrics*,' Ella said wistfully. 'Plum will be able to pick up all these fabulous designer knock-offs for like a few quid.'

'Made by starving little kids,' Lexie pointed out wryly. Her parents refuse to have anything in their house that isn't fairly traded. Lexie takes after them in having extremely strong principles. She and Ella occasionally fall out over this. Although Ella has a heart of gold, she tends to forget that everybody's life isn't just like hers and gets hurt and huffy when Lexie reminds her!

I saw her draw in a sharp breath. 'You say that like it's my *fault* the little kids are starving,' she said, then luckily our food arrived before she and Lexie could get into an argument.

'Oh, that looks *good*,' Lexie said greedily as Jools smilingly set down Lexie and Ella's plates. 'Smoked salmon, dill and new potato omelette for you two,' Jools said. She looked at me and Billie. 'Fruit salad, granola and Greek yoghurt for Billie and croque-monsieur for Natalie. Is that the right way round?'

'You know us too well,' I said, inhaling the delicious melted cheese and ham aroma of my croque-monsieur. The food at Mario's was always fabulous, but today we appreciated it even more because we'd had all those weeks to realise what we were missing.

When Jools had gone, I forked up a savoury mouthful, closing my eyes in bliss as I chewed, then I suddenly remembered the wedding and put down my fork. 'You know this is probably going to be my last proper meal?' I told my friends dramatically.

'How come?' asked Billie.

I pulled a face. 'On Monday evening we're going to

Gus's gym to meet his scary trainer, Jacek.'

'Hey, everyone can benefit from working out,' said Lexie crisply. 'It might do you good.'

I was in the middle of swallowing a mouthful and almost choked. I had a few desperate sips of my cappuccino, and finally recovered, but my voice still came out squeaky. 'Are you saying I *need* to drop two dress sizes?' Lexie is usually the first person to reassure me that my curves are natural, healthy and more than OK.

'You don't need to drop *any* dress sizes, you fool!' she said immediately. 'I'm just saying that everybody can benefit from a bit of a workout and you might actually have fun.'

'Yeah, Jacek might be really hot!' teased Ella.

'And if you genuinely hate it, fake an injury or something,' Lexie went on ruthlessly.

This might sound pathetic but I'd expected more sympathy from my friends. I didn't expect my family to understand, but I'd thought my friends would realise what a complete nightmare this was for me.

It was OK for Lexie. She's just naturally good at physical stuff but I am famously unco-ordinated (my nickname at boarding school was 'Un-co'), which when you're as tall as me is not funny. Now I was going to have to expose my lack of co-ordination in a public gym in front of my perfectly co-ordinated sisters, and my stepmother the former school hockey star. Of course, being a Bonneville-St John I didn't let on that this prospect turned my knees to jelly. 'Knowing me, I won't have to *fake* an injury. Ha ha ha,' I joked, but my quip came out sharper than I intended and Lexie blinked at me in surprise.

'Everything all right, girls?' Jools was suddenly smiling down into our booth.

'Everything is *perfect*,' Lexie said with feeling.

'Billie, I won't interrupt your get-together, but before you go could we have a quick chat. I'd like to run something by you.'

'Yeah, sure!' Billie sounded slightly surprised.

When Jools had gone Ella nudged her. 'I bet she's going to ask you to DJ.'

I do know that jealousy is not an attractive quality, but at that moment I felt so jealous of my friends I couldn't breathe.

I never realised how talented Billie was until we saw her perform her first ever set at the Grove fund raiser a few weeks ago. She sings, she writes her own songs, she plays guitar and keyboards, and she's a brilliant DJ. Billie's also a real beauty, though she is far too wrapped up in her music to think about her looks. Then there's blonde, beautiful Ella, who throws on the kookiest combinations of clothes yet always ends up with her own unique Ella Swanson brand of crazy-sexy-cool. Lexie is not a style queen like Ella, but people notice her because of all the positive energy that comes from her. She was unusually subdued today (for Lexie) but usually just five minutes with her makes me feel wide awake and ready for life.

And then there's me, the gawky ex-boarding-school girl with a major identity problem. Wouldn't you be jealous?

I finally came out of my thoughts to see Ella watching me with a sympathetic expression. 'Nat?' She made me look at her. 'What's up really? It can't just be your sister's wedding?'

I share a lot with my friends, more than I ever would have dreamed during my years of misery at boarding school. They know about my stepmum, they know about my sisters, they know I have the confidence of a tiny little newt, and that I'm still figuring out who I want to be. And I guess they half suspect my secret wish to be as beautiful and special as my three gorgeous friends. But *knowing* something is one thing, actually saying it out loud is something else.

I want to be beautiful like you. You see? Some things can't be told even to your closest friends. They hurt too much.

Billie and Ella must have sensed something though, because they exchanged glances and Ella leaned forward with a conspiratorial smile. 'So tell us all about this big wedding. I bet your stepmum is going to be in her element organising everybody in sight!'

I shook my head. 'Actually, I think Plum and Gus have pretty much got it all sorted. Gus doesn't want a church wedding so they're having it at his friend's hotel in Richmond. Apparently it's got gardens going down to the Thames. They're hoping to get the same caterers who catered one of the Spice Girls' weddings.'

Billie gave a splutter of laughter. 'The Spice Girls! That's going back!'

My sisters used to love the Spice Girls. That was before they hit their teens and turned middle-aged. I remembered them singing into their hair-brushes, wearing tiny trainer bras and waist slips, practising the sexy moves they'd seen in the pop videos. If they were in a good mood they'd let me be in their audience. I'm not sure but I think these song-and-dance sessions only happened when Jenny was out.

'So, who's doing the flowers?' Ella asked. She'd been

to loads of weddings so she was a bit of an expert.

'Gus's sister,' I said. 'She's a florist who specialises in weddings. Plum says she just opened a branch in New York.'

'This is starting to sound like a celebrity wedding!' Ella looked reluctantly impressed.

'Is that what you're going to have, Nat?' Billie asked with interest.

I shook my head. 'For one thing, I *seriously* doubt I will ever get married. But if I do, I'll just fly off to the Caribbean or somewhere with my fiancé and get married on the beach in front of a flock of seagulls.'

Billie looked shocked. 'You don't want anyone from your family there to see you married?'

'I'd want my dad to be there,' I admitted, 'but you can't have him without Jenny, and no way is Jenny going to be allowed to come anywhere near my wedding.'

'Seriously, Natalie? Is that really how you feel?' Ella's eyes were huge with dismay. 'That is *so* sad.'

'Not really,' I said carelessly. 'Like I said, I'm not likely to be getting married.' Then before my friends could ask any more searching questions I said brightly, 'So what kind of weddings are you guys going to have?'

'Actually, I've got a similar problem,' Ella said with a

sigh. 'Well, minus the wicked stepmother.' She gave my hand a sympathetic pat. 'I would love my dad to give me away and I'd love to have my little half-sister Kitty as a bridesmaid, but Mum would probably go ballistic. I'll have to sneak off to the Caribbean with you, Nat. We'll have a double wedding!' She gave us her sweet Ella grin but I could hear the sadness in her voice.

Ella's dad left Ella's mum to marry his PA, Naomi, and they now have a one-year-old baby. Ella still loves her dad and she gets on really well with Naomi, plus she adores little Kitty Saskia Honey, but Annie, Ella's mum, totally can't forgive him for leaving.

'Ells, by the time you get married your mum is bound to have mellowed,' Billie said, squeezing Ella's shoulder.

'You're being very quiet, Lexie? What kind of wedding are you going to have?' I asked curiously.

Lexie looked startled. 'Me? I don't know if I ever want to get married. I think I'd rather have fun.'

'Being married could be fun!' Billie waggled her eyebrows. 'You know, if it was with the right person!'

'It doesn't look like fun to me.' Lexie's voice had a sudden edge. 'VAT bills to worry about and hassles about whose turn it is to take out the rubbish or walk

35

the dog or pick up the kids. I think I'll pass.'

Lexie might be outspoken but she is usually the most positive person I know. We had never heard her sound so downbeat, and we totally didn't know what to say. Nobody wanted to come right out and ask if she was talking about her own parents in case we'd got it wrong, so there was an awkward silence that probably felt longer than it actually was. Billie gave me a desperate look; like, *You say something, Nat*!

'How about you, Billie?' I asked brightly to break the tension. 'Are you going to have a big wedding?'

She gave me a grateful smile. 'I want a real Notting Hill wedding, gospel choir, the works! I want my stepdad Mitch to give me away and my little brother Finlay to be my pageboy and I want this world-famous British designer Ella Swanson to design my dress.' She beamed at Ella. 'It's got to have an asymmetric hem and you've got to make me look sexier than Beyonce! Apart from that you can have totally free rein!'

Ella pretended to be scribbling these details on her napkin. 'Asymmetric hem, sexier than Beyonce. Got it!' she laughed.

'What kind of man are you going to marry though, Billie?' I asked with interest. It wouldn't have surprised me if she had picked him out already. Billie always gives the impression of knowing exactly what she wants out of life.

She didn't hesitate. 'Somebody like my dad; not Mitch, though I love him to bits. I mean like my real dad. He'll be a musician, handsome, funny.'

'Ooh, *Billy*!' everyone teased.

Even Lexie perked up. 'I just might fall in love with him myself,' she joked.

'So go on, what's his name!' demanded Ella.

We were all getting giggly now.

'I haven't met him yet!' Billie said, blushing. 'But I'll *definitely* know him when I see him!'

Jools came over to see what was going on. 'You girls sound like you're having fun!'

'Sorry. Were we being too noisy?' I asked anxiously.

She laughed. 'Natalie, we're Italians! When customers start getting noisy we feel like we must be doing something right!'

'We were just planning our weddings,' Ella explained.

'Nothing like a bit of forward planning!' Jools said, smiling. 'Actually, that's quite a coincidence. Louis and I have just decided to get married. We're thinking next June.' She held up her hand and for the first time we saw her engagement ring with its winking diamond.

'Oh my God, Jools!' Ella squeaked. 'That rock is HUGE!'

Billie jumped up and hugged her. 'I'm so happy for you both. Louis is so great! I'm really glad you're making it official.'

We all joined in congratulating her.

'So, have you decided what kind of wedding you're having?' asked Ella.

Jools laughed. 'You've met my dad, right? So you know it's got to be a big fat Italian wedding with all my aunties fighting over who gets to cook what, and there will be mountains of food and everyone will cry and my male relatives will all drink too much and fight over whatever it is men fight about.'

'That sounds like fun,' said Billie.

'It sounds tiring!' Jools said with a sigh. 'I'm tempted to just sneak off with Louis and get married on the quiet but that would break my dad's heart, so big fat Italian wedding here we come!' she said ruefully. 'Anyway, I didn't come over to talk about weddings. My dad asked me to tell you that he has made some fresh *dolce* especially in your honour.'

We gasped.

'Honestly?' said Ella. 'He actually made them just for us?'

We'd had them the very first time we came to Mario's. They were the most beautiful little pastries I'd ever tasted, like puffy little clouds filled with exquisite cream fillings.

'I can't believe he remembered!' I breathed.

Jools smiled. 'Papa remembers everything. I told him you might not have room but—'

'We have room!' everyone chorused at once.

'It's Nat's last meal,' Ella explained.

Jools tsked in sympathy. 'You're being shot at dawn, right?'

I pulled a face. 'As good as. I'm being a bridesmaid.'

'You're not going on a diet?' Jools sounded like she'd rather be shot.

I felt my face getting uncomfortably warm. 'It'll just be leading up to the wedding. My stepmother says I should do the Atkins diet.'

'If your stepmother think you need to go on a diet, Natalie, I'm sorry to say this, but she got a *serious* screw loose!' Mario had come up with a tray of light-as-air *dolce* in one hand and some evil-looking tongs in the other. 'You are beautiful just the way you are, my darling,' he added in a fierce voice. 'All you girls are so beautiful.'

All you girls are so beautiful.

It wasn't just what he said. It was the way Mario said it, like he really, truly meant it. 'I've only got to keep it up for two months,' I mumbled bashfully. 'Just so I can fit into my bridesmaid's dress.' I could feel my cheeks burning red now like poppies.

'Well, make sure you don't go crazy like these poor girls you see around Notting Hill, skinny little legs like twigs. After the wedding you come straight here to Mario's and let me feed you up with plenty pasta, you hear?'

I don't know why but when Mario said that about legs like twigs a picture of Sarah Corrie flashed into my mind. By the time her parents took her away from school, she'd got so shrunken and thin that her eyes looked massive in contrast, like a bush baby's. Luckily I knew that could never happen to me. I loved food too much!

We filled our mouths with the *dolce* and groaned with pleasure.

'Oh my GOD, I have SO missed this place!' Ella said.

'Has it really only been two months?' said Lexie.

We counted up; the terrible two weeks when we thought we'd lost Mario's for ever, plus six weeks to refurbish.

'It is only two months. But it feels like a lifetime,' I agreed.

We ordered more cappuccinos, and settled down for a gossipy catch-up. Like always, I felt all my troubles gradually melting away. Billie calls it 'Breakfast Club magic' and it works every time. Every Saturday morning we walk into Mario's as four different girls with totally separate lives, and by the time we walk out we're as close as sisters, at least like sisters are supposed to be.

I hope we stay this close for ever, I thought, but I didn't say it out loud. I was scared I might hex the most important thing in my life.

Chapter Three

'If you had been a cocker spaniel your stepmum would have liked you *much* better,' Lexie said once and we all laughed, though we knew it wasn't a joke.

The only time I saw Jenny cry was when Barkley got an inoperable tumour and she had to have him put down. To be fair to my stepmother she didn't have much experience with kids before she married my dad. One minute she was in rural Norfolk helping her widowed dad run his country estate, organising pheasant shoots for rich businessmen and breeding field spaniels and working cockers, next minute she was in Kensington Square giving dinner parties for my dad's colleagues and coping with three motherless girls.

I was fifteen months old when my mum died, also of an inoperable tumour, on her brain, and according to my sisters I was a total nightmare, dragging my disgusting pink blanky around with me everywhere and howling for my mummy. Plum and Nellie, being Plum and Nellie, were a different type of nightmare. They had always been bossy little girls but after our mother died they were like angry little witches, treating all Jenny's attempts to win them round with utter scorn and contempt.

According to Mrs Nolan our housekeeper (she didn't work for us then but she'd heard all the stories from our previous housekeeper, Mrs Meadows), my stepmother was on the verge of a nervous breakdown, when she came up with a genius idea. She asked my sisters if they would help her bring me up!

My sisters apparently decided that a time share in a real live baby was too good an opportunity to pass up because they jumped at it.

With their own baby to boss about whenever the fancy took them, Plum and Nellie quickly became reformed characters. They stopped pouring Jenny's perfume down the sink and putting dead snails on her side of the bed and became almost scarily well-behaved. Jenny was happy because she now had two fulltime snitches and informers; 'the Natalie Police' as my friends call them, which left her free for the important things in life like her dogs and playing bridge. Everyone was happy.

OK, obviously I wasn't *quite* so happy, but I adapted to my bizarre situation like little kids do. If Plum or Nellie said I couldn't have pudding for a week because I'd sneakily fed my poached eggs to one of the dogs (I still loathe and detest eggs in any form), that's just how it was. It was like being brought up by a committee; my three eagle-eyed mothers always watching to make sure I didn't slip up.

Now I was in my teens, and they still felt they had the right to comment on my looks, eating habits, posture. If we were having visitors, they'd insist on giving me an emergency 'makeover', straightening my naturally curly hair, squeezing me into those stupid magic knickers to hold in my curves, to make me more presentable.

My friends kept telling me that I had to stand up for myself and take back control of my life. They didn't understand that this was just how my family *was*. All I could do was just lie low like an escaping prisoner, hoping the searchlights would sweep over me, waiting till I could grow up and leave home.

'Can't you talk to your dad about them?' Ella asked me one time.

She couldn't see that my father isn't like hers. Even though she doesn't live with him now, Ella has a really close bond with her dad. My dad doesn't do 'close'. Maybe he was close to my mum before she died, but now he just works. He leaves for the City at five so he can get to his bank before the day's trading starts and he gets back as everyone else is going to bed. Even when he and Jenny throw one of their parties, you'll see him constantly checking his phone for messages.

The day that my dad took me to the steakhouse, must have been the longest conversation I'd had with him ever. It made me so happy that I got carried away with little fantasies of us doing stuff together, like a proper dad and his daughter. Most of my fantasies were set in Norfolk, where my family has a rambling old house called Pinchpots. My sisters and I still keep our ponies at some stables near there. I'd picture Daddy and me riding along the lanes as the sun set over vast frosty fields, then we'd go back to a wood fire and settle down to read or play some silly board game, just comfortable together, you know?

It never happened. Having come to my rescue, my dad immediately went back to his old habits, getting up early, coming home late and snacking on strange stinky cheese and biscuits before he went into his study to check the markets one last time, or whatever it is he does.

Mrs Nolan says he's like the Invisible Man. She says she only knows he's been home because she finds his cheese rinds and wrappers in the bin. But before my dad did his usual disappearing trick he did do one last good deed. He let me choose where I went to school. It's all thanks to Dad putting his foot down to Jenny that I met the other members of the Breakfast Club. With them for backup, I thought I might just survive. At home I lay low and did my best not to attract unwanted attention.

But now I had to be a bridesmaid, which was like the *opposite* of laying low! I'd have to walk down the aisle (or the corridor, whatever you walked down if you got married in a hotel) in front of *everyone*; ugly-duckling Natalie, the bright but not brilliant daughter who had to be brought home from boarding school because she didn't have the proper Bonneville-St John backbone. Being a bridesmaid might not be a big deal to Lexie, but it was a huge deal for me because there was absolutely no escape.

I spent all Sunday morning closeted in my room with my puppy, Betty.

I love my room. I love that it's right at the top of the

house so I always have advance warning when people are coming upstairs. My friends all say they'd find it spooky sleeping up here in an attic room all alone. Lexie says it's probably haunted by the ghosts of the poor underpaid servants that used to work for my Bonneville-St John ancestors long ago. Billie said she wouldn't sleep a wink in my room, not so much because of the ghost servants as that it's right next to the airing cupboard so you hear water constantly burbling and trickling. It's also a little small and a bit dingy and needs redecorating.

None of these things bother me. I think my room is perfect. It's got everything I need. I've got a desk that used to be my great-granny's. It's got little compartments where you can keep stuff. (I keep a supply of Betty's favourite gravy bone puppy biscuits in one.) I've got a fabulously romantic old bed that used to be great-gran's when she was a girl. Well, the brass bedstead used to be hers but my mattress is new. Sleeping on my long-dead great-grandmother's mattress would be too creepy even for me!

I've got two exquisite patchwork quilts that once belonged to my grandmother on my mum's side. They've both been patched and mended and the colours are slowly fading but to me that's all part of their charm. I think they're totally magic. One is all dark reds and deep blues and the other one is like creams and lilacs and soft blues and greys. Ella went mad with jealousy when she saw them. She kept saying, 'Have you any idea how much you could get for these down Portobello!' I told her, 'Why would I want to sell something so precious?'

My bed takes up most of my room. There's just enough space left for my chest of drawers and a curtained rail where I hang the clothes I wear most. The rest I keep in Nellie's wardrobe. Obviously like the other girls in the Breakfast Club I've got a pin-board. Like theirs, mine has pictures of me and my friends, some of them taken at Mario's. There are a couple of pictures of me riding my pony Saffron and dozens of pictures of Betty. Oh, plus a picture of the dishy young Judd Nelson. (Sigh.)

I also have a picture of Josh Berolli that I 'borrowed' from a school display, scanned into my computer then distributed to everybody in the Breakfast Club. Mr Berolli is like our secret crush. (That is, it's secret to everyone outside the Breakfast Club.) He's our new drama teacher and we all love him with a pure and undying love but I think it's fair to say that I love him the most. For a while I actually kept a file of fascinating Mr Berolli facts until I realised that it looked suspiciously like I was stalking him. I didn't fancy being the weird stalker-girl on top of being the ex-boarding-school loser who had panic attacks, so I stopped.

On my bedside table, I keep a framed picture of my mum when she was a little girl. I've got another very small picture of my mum and me together. It's really just a snapshot. I keep it inside my diary tucked out of sight in a drawer in my desk. Mrs Nolan found it a few years ago when she was spring cleaning and gave it to me. The photo was taken when I was still just a few months old. My mum is holding me high over her head and we're laughing into each other's faces as if we had all the time in the world to be together.

Because of all the precious things I keep in it, my room usually feels like my sanctuary, the one place in our house where I can relax and be myself. But today I felt strangely unsafe, like I was perched on a high narrow ledge that I might slip off at any moment. I couldn't stop thinking that today was my last real day of freedom. On Monday after school, the dressmaker who was making our wedding outfits, an old school friend of Plum's, was coming to our house. How Plum managed to swing that so soon after the wedding announcement I will never know. Then on Tuesday, after work, Plum was meeting us at a gym off the Harrow Road to meet the trainer who was allegedly going to transform me into a supermodel. I had started thinking of this as Operation Bridesmaidzilla because it seemed so epic – and also so unlikely.

'What do you think, Betty? Shall we tie all our possessions in a red spotty handkerchief and run away to sea?' I asked her miserably. 'Oops, I forgot that won't work. I get seasick.' Betty put her head on one side with her soft spaniel ears pricked, trying to understand what I was telling her. She looked so cute that I had to cover her with kisses.

Betty is the most adorable puppy in the world and she's totally mine. Jenny didn't give her to me. I took her. She was the runt of the litter and there's something slightly wrong with her front paws. It doesn't affect her at all but it means she can't be registered for the Kennel Club, which means she's no good for breeding.

Jenny adores dogs, but she's not the slightest bit sentimental about them. All her dogs are expected to pay their way. Her two spaniel bitches Tulip and Rosie each produce a litter of puppies every year, and as well as fathering all their puppies, her male dog Hamish is regularly put out to stud. It didn't make financial sense for Jenny to keep Betty however cute she might be so

Jenny decided to advertise her at a reduced price.

To our mutual surprise, I put my foot down. I told my stepmother that Betty could be all my birthday and Christmas presents until I left home, and she didn't have to buy me one other present *ever*, if that's what it took. Jenny was so startled she agreed. We called my puppy Betty after Ugly Betty, but she's not ugly. She's just ridiculously little, loveable and cute.

I always pray that nobody is bugging my room because then people would know just how mad I am about my dog. I call her the silliest names, telling her over and over in baby language how embarrassingly much I love her, then I'll whisper, 'This is just between us, Betty, OK? Nobody else must ever know!'

I picked her up for a cuddle and as usual she went nuts trying to lick me. My stomach rumbled. I looked at my watch. In the normal world it was almost time for lunch. Jenny said I could have as much protein as I wanted, but no carbs. As I'd feared, she'd put me on the Atkins diet. No carbs. That means no rice, pasta, bread, potatoes, no Krispy Kreme doughnuts, no delicious light-as-air *dolce* . . .

'It's just for two months,' I told Betty bravely as I set her back on her paws. 'You can *stick* anything for two months. We'll go downstairs and you can have your kibble and I'll have a Doctor Karg *cracker*, or something equally horrible, then I'll take you out to the park and by the time we get back home it will be almost time for some more protein. Yay!' Picking up on the new upbeat note in my voice, Betty did a hopeful little jump. 'Yay, protein!' I told her again, laughing.

I couldn't run away to sea so I'd have to find a way to cope. *Lexie's right*, I thought. *It's not such a big deal.* So what if I had to walk behind the bride and groom wearing a stupid pastel-coloured meringue. It was Plum's big day and I owed it to her not to show up like Bridesmaidzilla.

Next day I went to school having made a solemn vow that I wouldn't even mention the 'b' word once. I was going to be as calm and cool as if my sisters got married every day. OK, if someone asked me a direct question I would reply. Otherwise I would be a model of control and restraint.

As it turned out I didn't get the chance to do anything else! I found Ella by the notice board apparently mesmerised by a notice that had just gone up.

'Hi, Ells,' I said.

'Hey, Natz,' she said without turning round. 'Do you dare me?'

'Do I dare you to do what?'

53

'To enter Mrs Spelling's competition. Should I go for it?'

'Um, I might need a *tiny* bit more info,' I said, laughing. I'm your BF not your TTF! Totally telepathic friend,' I explained.

'Here, take a look!' Ella stepped back so I could read the notice that had gone up since last night. I immediately saw what had got her so excited. Our art teacher Mrs Spelling was inviting everyone in our year to enter a fashion design competition. The theme was 'School Days'. The entrants had to come up with designs for individual winter, summer and sports uniforms for our school. The winner would win a trip to Paris for two, all expenses paid.

The competition was made for Ella and I told her so.

'Suppose it isn't though,' she said anxiously. 'Suppose me breaking into fashion is just a sad little teenage dream and my designs are all rubbish?'

'They won't be rubbish,' I said confidently. 'You live and breathe fashion, Ella Swanson. You have this like weird fashion ESP.'

'What's with all the initials today!' she said, giggling. 'ESP is "extra" something or other, right?'

'Extra Sensory Perception,' I said. 'It's like a sixth sense. And you have it massively, Ella. You know what

54

colours and styles are coming in. You were *born* to do this, so *do* it, OK?'

'Oh, wow, thanks, Nat. You really mean it, don't you?' Ella looked like she might be going to cry.

I gave her a hug. 'I really mean it.'

'Group hug!' said Billie's voice behind us and her arms enveloped us both in a warm bear hug. 'Why are we hugging by the way?'

'Ella's going to enter Mrs Spelling's fashion design competition,' I explained.

'Oh, good call! That'll look good in your portfolio for St Martins',' Billie said at once.

'Only if I win,' Ella sighed.

'Yeah, well, you've got to be in it to win it, girl!' I could see a pleased little smirk tugging at the corners of Billie's mouth.

'I know that smile, Billie Gold. That's your good news smile,' I teased her.

Ella clapped her hands. 'Jools offered you the DJ slot! That's why she asked you to stay behind! You dark horse, how come you didn't say anything till now!'

Billie said she didn't want to talk about it until she'd run it past her mum, seeing as what happened last time. Billie's mum used to be a singer, something Billie only very recently found out. Until then Nina, her mum, had always seemed strongly opposed to the idea of Billie becoming a professional singer songwriter. Luckily the truth eventually came out and everyone is much happier. Billie and her mum have had some good heart to hearts and Billie has faithfully promised that she won't let her music interfere with her school work. She says that her stepdad Mitch is already boasting about his daughter the DJ. Billie said her mum obviously still feels super-protective of her but has agreed to let Billie take this golden opportunity.

'I can't believe I'm getting paid for doing something I love,' she marvelled. 'Plus it's Friday nights so I can give up my dishwashing job at pervy Ozzie's, yay!' Outside school, Billie juggles several part-time jobs, including dog walking and working on a market stall. I couldn't manage half of what Billie does in a day, and still keep up with my studies. I don't know how she does it.

'So how are you today, Miss Bonneville-St John?' she asked in a teasing voice. I felt a tiny glow of satisfaction that she had noticed me being unusually quiet.

'I'm *fine*!' I said cheerfully. 'The dressmaker's coming to measure us for our outfits tonight. So tell us about your set for Friday, Billie?' I said, quickly ducking out of the spotlight before I felt tempted to launch into my

Bridesmaidzilla shtick. 'Have you figured out what you're playing yet?'

At lunchtime I got another chance to practise my new low-profile personality on Oliver Maybury. I should probably explain about Oliver. He is a boy and yes he's my friend, but he is *not* my boyfriend. I've had to explain this to the others so many times that they now refer to him as NNBF. Not Nat's Boyfriend.

Oliver and I clicked in my very first week at my new school. He's tall and really sweet-looking, in an appealingly geeky way, with wild curly hair that looks like he belongs in one of those old 1970s movies. He's also freakily bright. I always tell my friends that he's the kind of boy who could probably hack into the Pentagon if he had to. 'But only if he *really* had to,' I explained to my astonished friends. 'Like if he had to save the world or something.'

Oliver and I immediately recognised that we shared the same weird sense of humour. We also both have a thing about cheesy old movies. Oh, and he loves to cook and I like to eat. That's pretty much the basis for our friendship.

When I am not with my Breakfast Club friends or up in my attic with Betty, you'll find me hanging out with Oliver at his mother's mews house in Portobello, just a couple of streets away from Ella's. Oliver's dad is something big in the Foreign Office but he doesn't live with them now. Oliver doesn't really talk about him. His mum is Fiona Maybury the documentary film maker. Her work means she is constantly travelling abroad. From what I've seen, Oliver and Louisa his six-year-old sister are quite often left to fend for themselves. There's an au pair, Eva, but judging from some of Oliver's stories, she needs more looking after than Oliver and Louisa put together!

I asked Oliver politely if he'd had a nice weekend and he said not really, he had to stay by the phone in case Eva's ex-boyfriend called.

'Why?'

'She said she didn't want to have anything to do with "that rat-bag",' he said, imitating Eva's German accent.

'You could have just unplugged the phone,' I suggested.

'We couldn't, in case Mom was trying to get through. She panics if she can't get hold of us.'

'Couldn't she just text you?'

'No, she's stuck on the border near Afghanistan. The guards took her mobile away along with her laptop and cameras,' Oliver said.

'Oh my God! Aren't you worried?' I gasped.

'Oh, she'll be all right,' he said calmly. 'Mum can talk her way out of most things. How was your weekend anyway?'

'OK. My sister's getting married and I'm going to be a bridesmaid,' I said in the casually cheerful tone I'd been practising.

Oliver frowned. 'Wow. So how do you feel about that, Natalie?'

'Oh, *fine*!' I said. 'Totally fine.'

'And what about your other sister, is she going to be a bridesmaid too?'

'There'll be three of us; me, Nellie and my little cousin Matilda.'

'So is Nellie happy about it?' Sometimes Oliver sounds like he's in training to make documentaries himself. I never knew a boy who asked so many questions.

I shrugged. 'I haven't actually asked her.' The truth was I'd hardly seen Nellie since Plum and Gus made their early morning announcement. She'd sipped at a glass of Gus's champagne, congratulated the happy couple then jumped in her little MG and zoomed off on some private errand of her own.

Over Oliver's shoulder, I could see Ella storming down the corridor looking like thunder.

'Ells? What's happened?' I said in dismay.

'Joe Grupetta happened,' she almost spat.

Joe Grupetta arrived at our school a few months before me. He's Maltese and really good looking if you can ignore his self-satisfied smirk. He's also good at art, though nothing like as brilliant as he makes out. I think being an 'artist' gives him the excuse to hang around the art room with Marie Louise and the Alpha Girls. The Alphas' real names are Danni, Pia and Isabella, and they are one of the reasons Billie and Ella took me under their wings that first morning. They are not exactly bullies. Bullying takes energy and all the Alpha girls are totally lazy. But they definitely see themselves as born to rule. I stay as far away from them as possible. They remind me too much of the McVeigh twins.

'What's Joe done now?' I asked Ella.

'He's only entering the fashion design competition,' she fumed.

'Why shouldn't he enter?' asked Oliver calmly. 'It's a competition!'

Ella gave him a frosty look. 'I don't mind that he *entered*, Oliver! I mind that he's telling everyone he's going to win! It's like the rest of us should just slink away and not even submit our inferior little designs.'

'Just ignore him, then,' Oliver said mildly. 'Success is the best revenge and all that.' He turned to me and gave a shy smile, then he loped away with his books under his arm to his advanced maths or science class or wherever he goes. My friends watched him disappear into the crowd with enigmatic expressions. I knew what was coming.

'Oliver *so* likes you, Natalie,' said Ella.

'He so does,' said Billie.

'I keep *telling* you—' I started, exasperated.

'We know what you keep telling us,' said Billie shaking her finger. 'We're just telling *you* that he *really* likes you.'

'No, he *really* doesn't, Billie! He's just a nice person, that's all.'

Billie's eyes sparkled with mischief. 'Hmm, maybe that's the problem? He's too nice. You prefer bad boys,' she teased.

'That's not true,' I protested. 'What about Josh Berolli?'

'Josh isn't a boy. He's a man,' Ella said, 'Anyway that's different. We all love Josh Berolli!'

'Sssh! Someone will hear you!' I hushed her.

'You're the one who brought him up!' Billie pointed out sternly. 'We were talking about Oliver Maybury and why you don't seem to notice that he's got a major crush on you.'

'She'd notice if he was Judd Nelson,' Ella said, giggling.

I swatted her. 'Shut up!'

'Speaking of Judd Nelson,' Billie whispered.

I broke into instant goose bumps. Tom Nash really does look spookily like the young Judd Nelson. He's got that same cool stare, as if he has the God-given right to look at anyone he wants, and the same floppy bad boy hair. Rumour has it that he was thrown out of his old school for smoking marijuana. He nodded unsmilingly at Ella and Billie as he sauntered past with his mates. He didn't nod at me but I never expected him to. I wasn't nearly cool or pretty enough to be on Tom Nash's radar.

I waited till my heart rate dropped back to normal then I said, 'So are you definitely entering the design competition, Ella?'

She brightened. 'I am! I just picked up the details from Mrs Spelling. I'm really doing it, Natalie! I'm so excited!'

That afternoon we had biology; not that Ella and Billie seemed to notice. Now and then I'd catch Billie humming under her breath as she scribbled down the name of another tune she'd thought of for her set. Ella started off dreamily doodling in the back of her exercise book. I sneaked a peek and grinned as I saw she'd just been doing her new favourite doodle over and over; the three tiny linked hearts that she plans to have as her logo when she's a bona fide fashion designer. All Ella's exercise books were covered with them. Half the time I don't think she knew she was doing it. The doodles must have just been a warm-up exercise while she was thinking because after a while she stopped drawing hearts and started busily sketching.

With my chin propped on my hands I forced myself to read about the different forms of pollination, while I secretly congratulated myself for staying so chilled about the wedding. Then the bell went for the end of lessons and I was instantly gripped by ice-cold panic.

You liar, Natalie, I scolded myself. I'd been lying to myself from the moment I opened my eyes. I had spent my entire day obsessively 'not thinking about the wedding', which was just a sneaky roundabout way of actually thinking about the wedding! And now I had to go home, where Plum's dressmaker friend was waiting to measure me for my bridesmaid's dress.

Chapter Four

When I walked in, the dressmaker, who was called Iris, was crawling around on the rug after my four-year-old cousin Matilda trying to get her measurements. It was taking a while because Matilda was incredibly ticklish. I'd always thought of Iris as an old lady's name but she was really young and chic in a close-fitting black tunic over leggings.

Jenny and Matilda's mother, my aunt Clare, were watching the fun from the sidelines. My stepmother was tapping her fingers against the arm of her chair, unamused. 'That child is out of control,' she said coldly as if my aunt wasn't there.

'If you think you can control her, Jenny, please go ahead!' my aunt offered cheerfully. Matilda is the youngest of her five children by ten years so she's more like an only child. I suppose she is a bit precocious (she learned to read before she was even three!) but I can't help loving Matilda. She's got a mop of wild, light brown curls, dark-lashed hazel eyes and a scattering of tiny freckles.

'Hi, Natalie!' she called, spotting me in the doorway. 'I'm going to be a bridesmaid just like you!'

'Assuming I ever catch her!' Iris commented breathlessly.

Plum was perching on the arm of an old faded chesterfield texting someone and wearing a harassed expression. 'At least *you're* here,' she grumbled when she saw me. 'Where *has* Nellie got to? She promised she'd get here early.'

'Matilda, stand still and let Iris do her job!' My aunt was starting to be annoyed. 'It was very kind of her to fit us in at such short notice so try to behave!'

'I was happy to fit you in,' Iris said. 'Plum's my oldest friend. It's just lucky I had a cancellation.'

'If I let you measure under my arms, will you make me look "as beautiful as the day"?' Matilda asked Iris with interest. 'In stories they always say that princesses are "as beautiful as the day".'

'Making you beautiful isn't actually going to be too hard, sweetie,' Iris said, laughing. 'That is a great outfit she's wearing by the way,' she told my aunt. 'I especially like the fairy wings with the wellies!'

'She dressed herself,' said my aunt with a sigh.

To everyone's relief, Matilda finally allowed herself to be measured and my aunt rewarded her with a tube of Love Hearts. Then Mrs Nolan came in with tea things on a tray and Ada gratefully took a break.

Betty, who had been shut away in the kitchen, took this opportunity to escape to join in the fun. She instantly made a beeline for Matilda and started jumping up excitedly. 'No, Betty! Down, bad puppy! Love Hearts aren't good for dogs! Don't worry, Jenny!' Matilda called cheerfully to my stony-faced stepmother. 'I'm keeping them out of her way like this, look!'

'Betty, sit down this *minute* or you'll go in your crate!' I said in my sternest voice. Poor Betty sat down so fast that her ears actually bounced. 'Good girl,' I said in a gentler tone.

Matilda blew out her breath. 'Thank you, Natalie. My arm was getting really tired.' She carefully took out a Love Heart and gave it to me, warm and sticky from her hand. 'That's for you. It says "U R a Babe",' she said gravely. 'That means you're like a *really* cute girl that all the boys like!'

'Yep, that's me, the cute girl that all the boys like,' I said with a sigh. I was about to pop the sweet in my mouth when I felt an icy vibe from my stepmother's side of the room. 'I'd love to,' I said, regretfully returning her sweet. 'But I'm actually on a diet.'

'You don't need to be on a diet!' said Matilda, surprised.

'Thank you!' I said gratefully. 'But I need to look my best for Plum's wedding.' I tried to smile, but with my stepmother listening to every word we said it probably looked more like a sick grimace.

'You *do* look good already,' Matilda insisted. 'When I grow up I want to be just like you, Natalie!'

I saw my stepmother's mouth tighten and braced myself for a sour remark, but just then my sister Nellie walked in wearing her smart work clothes. Nellie works for a big Swiss bank in the City, which is where she met Rupert.

'What happened to *you*!' Plum demanded angrily. 'You promised you'd get here early to help me choose fabrics.'

'Excuse me for having a life!' Nellie snapped. 'I got held up. OK? Can you do me next?' she asked Iris. 'I'm meeting someone in an hour and I need to shower and change.'

'No problem,' Iris said, smiling, and she whisked over with her notepad and tape-measure.

'But what about the fabrics!' Plum wailed.

'Oh, Plum, for heaven's sake! Just show me the ones you like and I'll see if I agree.'

'But what if I'm wrong?' Plum quavered. 'This is a big thing for me, Nellie, a *really* big thing!' She suddenly sounded about the same age as Matilda. I think it's the first time in my life that I'd ever felt sorry for her. Even Nellie's expression softened. In that moment everyone totally understood who my sister really wanted here with her to help choose the material for her wedding dress and it wasn't Nellie or Jenny. It was our mother.

Nellie and Plum put their heads together over the swatches of exquisite snowy white silks. Plum showed Nellie the sample she'd picked out for the bridesmaids' dresses (a subtle silvery grey); and to Plum's obvious relief they both agreed. Then Iris measured my sister's tiny size-six frame; jotting down the figures, and Nellie raced off to get ready for her date. Iris turned to me, smiling. 'You must be Natalie? Don't look so worried, I promise not to bite!'

Five minutes later I was in my room face-down on my bed bawling like a two-year-old. I wasn't a size six. I wasn't even a size eight. Iris didn't comment on my appalling measurements. She was much too professional as well as too kind, but my stepmother made a point of reading them silently over her shoulder and I heard her make a sound of disgust. I fled from the room before she could say, 'I told you so.' I didn't even stop to pick up Betty.

I'm not sure how long I'd been up there sobbing, maybe half an hour, when Nellie suddenly barged in. I'd been crying so hard I hadn't heard her come up the stairs. I quickly sat up, scrubbing my hands across my eyes. 'I thought you'd got a date?'

She pulled a face. 'I wasn't in the mood. Plum said you went rushing off. What's up?'

'Nothing's up. I've got a history essay to write, that's all,' I fibbed.

I saw Nellie look around my room, where there wasn't a history book to be seen. 'So you're not – um – upset because of your measurements?'

'Lord no!' I did a surprised laugh, quickly swiping any leftover tears and snot off my cheeks.

'Because if it *was* that . . .'

'I'm *not* upset,' I said, defying her to mention my red swollen face.

'I mean a wedding is really just like a super-sized party. It would be silly to get upset about a party.'

'I totally agree,' I said. 'But like I told you, I'm not upset.'

Nellie hovered in the door as if she didn't know whether she should stay or go. 'Well, if you're sure,' she said awkwardly and barged out as suddenly as she'd come in.

I have a washbasin in my room and after Nellie had gone I carefully washed and dried my tear-stained face. Then I saw my face in the small square of looking glass over the basin, and the humiliation hit me all over again.

After a while I heard Mrs Nolan come puffing up the stairs. 'Your sister said you might not be down for supper. She says you have an important essay to write, so I've brought you a little snack on a tray.' She had brought me a bowl of homemade soup, a slice of toast, and an apple.

I felt my face start to crumple all over again. I love Mrs Nolan and I know she loves me. She can't show it too blatantly because my parents are her employers, but she constantly does thoughtful little things to let me know she cares. She had even put my soup in the pretty blue-rimmed bowl I always use if I'm eating by myself. It's the kind of thing your mother might notice and I think that's why Mrs Nolan did it. It distressed her that I didn't have a mother who really cared about me, so whenever she could she tried to fill the gap.

As usual, Betty had exploited the fact that our housekeeper had her hands full, by sneakily following her up the stairs and jumping up on my bed, where she pretended not very convincingly to go to sleep. 'Don't even *think* of sending me back downstairs,' her expression seemed to say. For such a little puppy Betty has strong opinions.

Mrs Nolan seemed to be fumbling for something in her apron pocket. She looked angry suddenly. 'Your stepmother wanted me to give this to you along with a message and that's the only reason I'm doing it. But I'm not happy about it, Natalie, not happy at all.'

I swallowed. 'What's Jenny's message?'

'She said—' Mrs Nolan's voice shook. 'She said maybe now you'll see why you can't go on eating everything you fancy like a greedy little—' She couldn't bring herself to say the word.

'Pig,' I whispered. My stepmother had called me a lot of things in her time but calling me a pig was an all-time low.

Mrs Nolan was so upset she couldn't look me in the eye. She just went out, leaving a well-used paperback next to the tray with my supper. I recognised it from across the room. *The Atkins Diet.* I knocked it to the floor, kicking it under my bed until it was totally out of sight. Then I sat carefully spooning up Mrs Nolan's soup, dipping in tiny pieces of dry diet toast, feeling like an invalid. When my bowl was polished clean, I switched on my laptop to see if any of my friends were around for a chat. I didn't want to tell them my troubles. (Why would you want to tell someone your stepmother just called you a pig?) I only wanted to escape and forget what had happened.

To my surprise *Lexie's* name popped up in a chat box.

Lex: *Hi*

These days, what with her skating, her school work, and all the chores she has to do at home, Lexie is usually way too busy to chat online.

Hi, I typed. *How's things at your house?*

Lex: *weird*

This didn't sound like our Lexie. *Weird how?* I typed.

Lex: *Its just a weird vibe, Dad seems really down, plus Kathy's started working from home.*

Lexie's parents run an organic veggie business called Sweet World. Usually they work together at their unit on a local industrial estate where they make up boxes of veggies that they later deliver all around Notting Hill.

Natz: *did you ask her why?*

73

Lex: *she said she needed to catch up on admin, plus she thought I deserved a break from my brothers, but I don't think that's it.*

Natz: *what do you think it is?*

After a long pause a new chat-box popped up.

Lex: *one nite i heard them fighting when i was in bed, i'm scared they mite split up.*

Nobody wants to lie in bed listening to their parents fighting. I felt really sorry for Lexie. I just wished I knew what to say to make her feel better. Billie and Ella are way more experienced agony aunts than me. But Lexie had told her troubles to *me*, I thought with a flicker of pride, so I would just try my best.

Natz: *it's prolly nothing, all parents fight sometimes.*

Not my parents obviously. Jenny and my dad never fight, possibly because Daddy is hardly ever home. *I bet they're just stressed about bills and stuff, it's just a phase, Lex, it'll blow over and everything will be fine again.*

Lex: *ur not just saying that?*

Natz: *no, I really mean it.*

Lex: *ur right, i was just being silly.*

Natz: *u aren't silly. Plus hav u noticed, worries are worse at nite!*

Lex: *I know, i wonder why that is? thanks for listening nat, ur a good friend, how's u anyway?*

Natz: *i'm fine!* I fibbed. *just going 2 cuddle up with betty, nite nite!*

I logged off and went to brush my teeth, then I climbed into bed and switched off my lamp. I lay staring into the darkness for a few minutes, then I sat up and switched my lamp back on and got out of bed. The diet book had travelled surprisingly far under my bed and took a while to fish out. The minute I had it in my hand I dropped it again as if I'd been scalded.

'What are you scared of, Natalie?' I whispered. It wasn't like Dr Atkins himself was going to come billowing out of its pages like the Evil Dieting Guru and physically force me to follow his diet. *It's just information*, I reminded myself. Information was something you could take or leave. I could read it, weigh up the pros and cons, and make up my own mind.

I snatched up the book and took it back to bed feeling as ashamed and self-conscious as if people were watching me on reality TV.

An hour later my head was spinning with facts and figures. I hated to admit this but it seemed like my stepmother's best buddy Dr A. had all the necessary knowhow to make me thin and pretty.

Could I do it though? Did I seriously have the

willpower to stick to all his weird dietary rules? I mean *really* stick to them, day in, day out, for the next two months? It didn't seem like I had a choice. Another hot wave of shame washed over me as I remembered my stepmother tutting at my monstrous measurements. I never wanted to feel that helpless ever again. I wanted to be in control of my body and my life.

It suddenly occurred to me that I had never felt like I was in control of anything, except maybe the little puppy which now lay snoring gently in my arms. *You trained Betty*, I reminded myself. In just a few weeks, I'd taught her to sit. I'd taught her to wait to eat from her bowl until I gave the command. I'd *almost* taught her to stop jumping at people. I was still working on training her to walk to heel. You just had to be really firm and keep plugging away. Jenny said you had to be clear in your own mind that your dog was going to obey you. Maybe I just had to get *really* clear in my own mind that I was going to lose weight? I had to retrain my body not to want high-calorie foods like sugary doughnuts and buttery pasta.

I lay in the dark stroking Betty's silky ears and imagining the incredibly slimming breakfast I would make for myself when I got up tomorrow. Dr Atkins said you could have cottage cheese. He recommended mixing a few spoonfuls with some thawed forest fruits. That sounded really nice, I thought, yawning, almost like dessert! Mmm, *dessert* . . . !

Images of illicit fruit puddings followed me into my dreams where Jools and Mario kept bringing an endless procession of outrageous Italian desserts. 'Eat them *all*!' Mario insisted, beaming. 'They have *minus* calories! I made them just for you, darling!'

When I came downstairs next morning I was totally gutted when I realised there were no forest fruits in our freezer. But I quickly told myself this was no reason to weaken. I had made a decision and I was going to stick to it. Since the forest fruits option was out I would calmly make do with a going-off banana from the fruit bowl. Cottage cheese and going-off banana is not the nicest combo but I eventually managed to force it down.

Jenny came in and instantly clocked what I was eating. 'Oh, my goodness!' she exclaimed sarcastically. 'I see you decided against your usual four slices of toast.'

'Hmm?' I said dreamily as if I really hadn't noticed. 'Oh, yeah, I didn't feel like toast this morning for some reason.'

'Don't forget to take some lunch,' she said. 'Otherwise

you'll make unwise dietary choices.' 'Unwise dietary choices' to Jenny meant anything that had a calorie, but especially chips. Lexie said it was probably because state-school kids eat them. 'Chips are *full* of working-class calories, Natalie!' she had fluted brilliantly, taking off my stepmother's voice. 'What *would* William and Kate think if they found out!'

I gave Jenny my most insincere smile. 'I know, I was really worried about making bad choices too, so I packed some Dr Karg crackers and plenty of cucumber!' I patted my school bag as proof. I was lying of course. I hadn't packed any lunch. After the wedding I could eat as much lunch as I wanted. For now my goal was to fit into my bridesmaid's dress without shaming myself or my sister. If I could annoy the hell out of my stepmother at the same time, so much the better. I slung my bag over my shoulder and flashed another bright smile. 'Have a lovely day, Jenny, won't you!'

Just for a moment my stepmother looked confused. It was like she knew something had changed between us but she wasn't sure what. I was still smirking to myself as I ran to catch my bus. For the first time, possibly since Jenny married my father, I'd had a taste of power.

Chapter Five

At lunchtime, we grabbed our usual table and sat down.

Ella absent-mindedly spooned up pasta salad out of a little pot, while she flicked through the new designs in her notebook.

Billie was worrying out loud about her set at Mario's. 'I mean it's a great opportunity. But am I actually ready? I mean, *really* ready? What do you think, Nat?' she asked, seeing that Ella was obviously miles away.

'Me?' I said, surprised. 'Well, I'm not the world expert on DJ readiness as you know, but I think you should probably just dive in and then I suppose you'll kind of *have* to be ready?'

Billie looked impressed. 'Thanks, Nat, I think you could be right! Like *Feel the Fear and Do it Anyway*— that's an old self-help book of my mum's,' she explained, grinning.' I've never read it. But every time I see the title on the shelves it gives me a major boost!'

It seemed like I'd picked the perfect day for my not eating lunch experiment. Neither of my friends seemed to notice that all I'd had was an occasional sip of Sprite. When Billie moved on to fretting about whether she should put this tune or that tune in her set, I began to relax. I should have remembered that Billie Gold notices *everything*. 'Where's your lunch, girl?' she demanded abruptly. 'We've been here fifteen minutes and you haven't even cracked open your lunch box!'

'I didn't actually bring any. I overslept,' I fibbed. 'I just grabbed my bag and ran for the bus.'

'Why didn't you *say*!' Billie said immediately. 'Here have a couple of my chicken sandwiches. I made too many anyway.'

At the word 'chicken' my stomach gave a hopeful growl but I coughed to cover it. 'Thanks but I don't actually feel that hungry.'

'You're not getting sick?' she asked anxiously.

'Hey, I'm as healthy as a horse, you know me!' I said, laughing. 'It's just butterflies.'

Ella looked up from her notebook with a smirk. 'She's nervous about meeting her sexy personal trainer, aren't you, Natalie?'

'Shut up!' I said. 'I've never been to a gym before that's all.'

'I wonder if you'll see any celebs?' Ella mused.

'If there are celebs involved I'm coming with you!' Billie joked. She put away her uneaten chicken sandwich and took out her yoghurt.

My mouth started to water. I almost weakened and begged for the sandwich. *Willpower, Nat,* I reminded myself and I went on taking occasional tiny sips of Sprite as I told my friends about my online conversation with Lexie.

'I did kind of wonder when she said that about not getting married,' said Ella.

'We all did,' Billie said, sighing. 'Actually last time I was at their house Will was a bit—' She frowned. 'I don't know. Something about him didn't feel right.'

'I hope they aren't going to get a divorce,' said Ella anxiously. 'That would kill Lexie.'

'*Your* parents divorced and you survived,' Billie pointed out.

'Oh, I survived!' she stressed, sounding unusually fierce for Ella, 'like you and your mum survived your dad leaving, Billie. But nobody *wants* it to happen to them, right?'

'No,' Billie agreed soberly. 'Nobody wants it to happen.'

'I mean if my dad had like, died in a train crash,' Ella went on, 'instead of falling in love with Naomi, my mum would probably still be saying nice things about him. Instead she spits flames if I so much as mention his name.'

'My mum died. Nobody mentions her at all,' I pointed out. I don't usually mention my mother either and immediately wished I could take it back.

'Your family is a special case though, you have to admit,' said Billie.

She sounded so normal about it that I didn't feel so bad about bringing up my long-dead mother in the dinner hall. 'That's such a nice way of saying we're all totally screwed up,' I said gratefully.

'Oh, Nat, come on! Practically every family we know is totally screwed up!' said Ella.

'Maybe that's why we don't want Lexie's parents to get a divorce,' Billie suggested. 'Lexie's the only one of us four who has the exact same set of parents she started out with. We'll probably be getting married one day. We want to believe we've got a cat in hell's chance of living happily ever after!'

'Sure we do – have a cat in hell's chance, I mean,' said Ella, who is basically a glass half full girl.

'I told Lexie it was just a phase,' I said guiltily. 'I said they were probably worried about money and it would blow over and everything would be fine.'

Billie frowned. 'You say that like you got it wrong.'

'I might have,' I said. 'I didn't know what to say to her. You'd have said exactly the right thing, Billie. I know you would.'

She looked torn between exasperation and pity. 'Will you just give yourself a break! There's been *enough* times when someone's in trouble that I didn't have a clue what to say, but like you I was the girl in the hot seat so I just did my best. You did your best, honey! I'm sure you said exactly what Lexie needed to hear.'

'Totally,' Ella agreed warmly. 'She just needed you to be there, and you were.' She scraped out the last of her pasta and I tried not to watch.

At last lunch break was officially over and we all headed towards the art room for double art with Mrs Spelling. On the way, Billie stopped to chat with Fareeda. Outside the art room, Joe Grupetta was in a huddle with Danni, Isabella and Pia, the Alpha Girls, and his annoying but extremely pretty friend, red-headed Marie Louise. Tamsin was hanging around tensely on the edge of their conversation as usual, waiting for her chance to be indispensable so the Alphas would finally accept her into their magic circle. Tamsin is not a stupid person so it's puzzling the way she doesn't get that this is never going to happen.

Ella and I went to bag a table. I was pleased to see that Mrs Spelling had set up a still life of apples and pears. Some people think still lifes are boring but I think they're kind of peaceful.

I noticed Ella's hand straying towards the folder that held her sketches. She looked around to make sure nobody else had come in. 'Would you mind looking at some designs I did last night?' She seemed almost shy about asking. 'They're very rough.' She did a nervous giggle. '*Extremely* rough actually!'

'These are your actual designs for the competition?' I was surprised and impressed. 'Wow, how keen are you!'

'I know. I surprised myself!' she said, laughing. 'I went home and just started drawing like a demon. Mum called me twice for my supper and I didn't even hear. It's like I'd gone into some kind of trance.' She pulled a face. 'I just can't tell if they're any good.' She flipped open the folder then immediately flipped it shut, half laughing at herself. 'I'm not sure if I dare show you now.'

'Show me the sketch you like best,' I suggested.

'Just that one?' she asked, surprised.

'Yeah, just that one,' I said cunningly. 'Just one

sketch can't hurt!'

'And you'll honestly tell me if it's rubbish?'

I nodded. 'Cross my heart. But it won't be.'

It wasn't. It was just a rough sketch of a design for a girl's summer top and skirt. It was simple and elegant and managed to be young and cool but in a way that wouldn't easily date.

Billie came to join us. 'Nice,' she said approvingly. '*Very* nice. Let's see the others then, Ella.'

Ella had turned pink with pleasure. 'You really think it's OK?'

'I love it,' Billie said sincerely. 'Now stop holding out on us, girl, and show us the rest!'

Ella nervously brought out the rest of her designs and we studied them carefully, telling her what we liked most about them. Suddenly Billie spun around with a banshee yell that made me and Ella jump out of our skins! 'Hey! Who invited you to go poking your sticky beak in, Joe Grupetta!'

I looked up to see him freeze in the middle of craning across the tables to get a look at Ella's designs. Next minute his smirk was back in place and I saw him whisper something to Marie Louise. But I had seen his expression as he clocked Ella's drawings and he didn't look happy.

Flustered, Ella quickly put her designs away.

'I never knew Joe was interested in fashion,' I hissed. 'It's a bit weird if you ask me.'

'You mean because he's a boy?' she said.

I shook my head. 'Not just that.'

'Most top designers are men,' Ella said. 'It's not so weird.'

I was fuzzy-headed from skipping lunch, and wasn't up to explaining what I meant. I hadn't meant it was weird because Joe was a boy. I thought it was weird because unlike Ella he obviously didn't have any real passion for fashion. I had a feeling he saw it as a shortcut, a shortcut to being our school's Mister uber cool.

Mrs Spelling had showed up by this time and I spent the rest of the afternoon happily messing about with coloured pastels, making peaceful pictures of apples and pears. Then it was time to go to the Harrow Road to meet Jacek.

Nellie and Plum were making their own way from work so Jenny and I had to go together. I'd thought we'd just go on the bus but Jenny said the Harrow Road, which is just up from Notting Hill, was notoriously rough and she'd feel safer in the Range Rover.

Sometimes I think Jenny forgets that she doesn't still

live in Norfolk. I think she assumed she'd be able to park right outside the gym and just zoom straight in, without making eye contact with the locals. This being London the only space we could find was up a dodgy looking cul-de-sac between seedy offices and a couple of old warehouses that had so far escaped being converted into super-trendy apartments.

I was relieved just to stop driving in circles and just wanted to get out of the car. By this time I was feeling distinctly queasy with hunger. But Jenny had seen a suspicious hoodie-wearing guy in a doorway and was in two minds whether to park. (He was wearing a hoodie, therefore he was obviously plotting to steal her car. That's honestly how my stepmother's mind works.)

I thought about Billie, who walks through the streets of Ladbroke Grove without turning a hair and is on first names with everybody around there. Jenny wouldn't even make eye contact with them. Unlike my stepmother, I have an open mind, though I probably wouldn't walk around here after dark.

Jenny finally locked the car, glaring around at any unseen hoodies who might be watching. Then she gripped on to my arm and made me practically run the few hundred metres to Jacek's gym which was actually in a converted warehouse. We were buzzed through to the downstairs foyer, where Plum was waiting minus Nellie. We waited there for a further ten minutes while other gym users went in and out, clutching bottles of mineral water.

'Doesn't my sister realise how lucky we were to even get a *sniff* of an appointment with Jacek!' Plum fumed as we waited. 'He's booked up for months ahead. We only got in because Gus pulled strings.'

'Is Jacek really that good?' I asked, trying to imitate Plum's pronunciation of our trainer's name; Yatcheck.

'Gus says he's a genius.' Plum was so stressed she was biting her lip. 'Came over from Poland with nothing and now he's got his own fitness empire. Amazing.' She checked her mobile in case Nellie had sent a text.

'Maybe we should just go in?' I suggested. After some more lip-chewing Plum decided we should wait another five minutes but at that moment Nellie showed up, not seeming the least concerned about keeping everyone waiting.

Plum led the way upstairs to a bright airy space where a pretty receptionist sat gossiping with a girl who looked as if she might be one of the other trainers. 'We've come to see Jacek,' Plum said in her boarding-school voice when no one acknowledged us. 'My name is Plum Bonneville-St John.'

The receptionist swallowed her mouthful of Twix, chucked the remains in a drawer, checked our names and picked up her phone. 'I'll tell Jacek you're here.' She spoke briefly on the phone then gave us a big smile. 'He says to go through.'

'*She's* not a very sparkling advertisement for health and fitness,' Nelly quipped as we followed Plum through the double doors into the gym. I had expected blaring music. In movies gyms usually had deafening pop pumping through the air to inspire gym users to push their muscles faster and harder, but Jacek's gym was as hushed and solemn as a church. The only sound was the soft whirring of machines and the occasional grunt of effort. This meant that Nellie's remark came out louder than she probably intended.

Plum gave her a sharp look and Nellie said innocently, 'What?'

'If you're not going to take it seriously,' Plum hissed.

Nellie hissed back, 'Plum, I'm *here*, aren't I? In what way am I not taking it seriously?'

My stepmother and I both pretended that we hadn't noticed my sisters were bickering again. Until Plum announced her wedding plans, she and Nellie had seemed as thick as thieves. Even when they both found long-term boyfriends they regularly spent time together, in fact the couples often went out as a foursome. But since Plum announced her engagement Nellie seemed to be hanging out more with people she knew from work and was only rarely at home. Probably this was just as well because when my sisters did get together, like now, the fur started to fly.

My stepmother stood examining her fingernails, with that mask-like expression she has as if everything is totally under her control, and I tried to look fascinated by the array of machines. Some I recognised as high-tech versions of the stationary bikes, steppers and rowing machines my sisters had bought and thrown away over the years. Others looked like instruments of torture.

While Nellie and Plum hissed at each other like well-bred snakes, I watched one woman pounding along on her high-tech treadmill to nowhere. She kept her eyes fixed straight ahead as if she was totally alone and not surrounded by other pounding, pedalling, sweating, grunting humans.

You could tell this was a super-posh gym, I thought, as my sisters continued to bicker, because it smelled amazing – of polished wood and another spicy, flowery smell that reminded me of the kind of expensive smells that came wafting out of Jo Malone's or Miller Harris.

'Ladies?' said a quiet, eastern European voice. Jacek had silently materialised beside us. Until I saw our personal trainer for real I didn't realise I'd been expecting a muscle-bound guy with a designer suntan and a dazzling fake smile. Jacek was the complete opposite of that muscle-bound guy. He was slim, wiry and pale with startlingly green eyes. He never smiled at us once. (Jacek and smiling didn't really seem to belong in the same sentence.) But his eyes held a cool glint of something that made me feel the tiniest bit flustered.

'Your gym smells lovely,' I babbled.

'Yes,' he agreed. 'I am not fond of the smell of rubber and sweat myself! Shall we go into my office and talk? Then I will show you around.'

In his office, Jacek asked us questions about our height and weight and levels of fitness. We all had to breathe into a little tube to see if our lungs were working properly. He said my lungs were perfect!

'So they should be at her age,' said my stepmother sourly.

Next we had to do simple resistance exercises, pushing against his arms so he could figure out what was going on with all our different muscle groups.

When it was Nellie's turn he commented, 'Oh, you are surprisingly strong!'

'For a girl, you mean?' she snapped.

'Of course not for a girl,' he said calmly, 'My grandmother was as strong as a horse; my mother and sisters too. I meant for someone so slender.'

'Oh,' said Nellie and you could see all the bad temper go out of her like air from a balloon.

Jacek said that now he had all our details he would be able to work out a personal programme for each of us so that we could be as slim and toned as possible for Plum's wedding.

'Plum says you can make us drop two dress sizes,' Nellie said in a disbelieving voice.

'I can't *make* you do anything,' he assured her. 'It is completely down to you if you drop the weight. I can only give you the benefit of my experience and teach you how best to help yourself and your body. That is assuming you feel it's necessary to lose so much weight,' he added. 'Myself I wouldn't—'

'A girl can never be too thin!' My stepmother interrupted with a laugh.

'That is certainly an opinion,' Jacek said coolly. 'Now let me show you around the machines. Don't worry that you won't remember everything from today. I will be happy to explain everything to you again when you come for your sessions.'

'We will definitely be seeing you every time?' Plum still seemed anxious that we might get palmed off with one of Jacek's less experienced trainers. 'My fiancé *specifically* said we would be working with you.'

Jacek pushed back his chair. 'It will be my pleasure to give all you ladies my personal attention at this very important and stressful time.'

'Oh, *thank* you,' Plum gushed.

I was starting to see why Jacek's gym was now *the* gym in Notting Hill. He might not be the most smiley man in the world but he was *really* charming.

I turned to see how Nellie was taking all this but she was frowning at the motivational posters behind Jacek's desk. One said: *A ship is safe in harbour but that's not what ships are for*. The poster next to it said: *When life gives you lemons, make lemonade*. Nellie felt me looking at her and gave me one of her poisonous looks. 'What?'

I just shook my head. Hopefully Rupert would ask her to marry him really soon then she'd leave home as well – except that would leave me alone with Jenny. Despite my perfect lungs, this thought immediately made me feel like I couldn't breathe.

Before we left, Jacek took us on a tour of the machines. I could feel the other gym users watching, jealous because we had his personal attention.

My heart suddenly skipped a beat. 'Isn't that—?' I started, but Jacek silently hustled us past so that I knew to contain my un-cool excitement at seeing a real live TV star slogging away on one of his steppers.

He relented as soon as we were out of earshot. 'Did you see her on *Strictly*?' he asked me. 'She came to my gym every morning at 5 am for six weeks to get fit before filming even started.'

'I never watch *Strictly Come Dancing*,' I said apologetically.

'I saw her,' said Plum, smiling for the first time since we'd arrived at the gym. 'She looked incredible, like a supermodel. And she actually came here to your gym?' Even Nellie had perked up at this news.

That's when I felt a rush of excitement so strong that I almost yelled. There's a word for this particular experience I was having that I only remembered later. Mr Berolli occasionally uses it in drama when a character suddenly understands something huge that she never understood before: 'epiphany'. I was having my first ever epiphany and it made me want to clap my hands and laugh and shout.

When life gives you lemons, make lemonade!

That was it! For the first time I totally got what that saying meant. 'Lemons' were all those disturbing unwanted things that come into your life. Like for instance I hadn't wanted to be a bridesmaid, and I definitely didn't want to go on the Atkins diet and I wanted to have a personal trainer like I needed a hole in the head. I could go on sulking about all my 'lemons' or I could adopt a shiny new attitude. I could tell myself; 'Natalie, life has sent you these lemons (the wedding, my monster measurements, Dr Atkins, Jacek and his scary gym) for a reason!' Then I could turn them all into lemonade!

Instead of seeing these things as my torturers, I could welcome them as my *helpers*, who had the power to turn me into the slim beautiful girl I had always longed to be!

I didn't hear a thing anybody said after that. I was totally dazed by this extraordinary revelation. I never really 'got' willpower before. For instance I'd always believed that I was too wussy to be like Lexie getting up at five so she could practise her figure skating at an almost empty ice rink. But for the first time, at Jacek's gym, I got it. It was so simple I couldn't believe I hadn't seen it before. You just had to *stick* with something and eventually you'd get results! If I kept up the cottage cheese and worked out with Jacek my body would do the rest. I'd be toned and fit in no time. I could be as fit as Lexie if not fitter. I would float through Plum's wedding looking as beautiful as the day. I couldn't *wait*!

Chapter Six

That night I went online to see if Lexie was up for a chat. I was going to tell her she'd been right; working out was definitely going to do me good.

I also wanted to boast about seeing a well-known TV star using the machines, but Lexie wasn't online. I'd been right about Kathy and Will, I thought. It had just been a phase like I'd told Lexie, and they'd made it up. Now the Brown family was sitting around in their big cosy kitchen playing a game of Scrabble? This thought made me feel suddenly lonely. Lexie had a real family that actually did things together, not a stepmother, two super-critical sisters and a disappearing Dad.

I realised I had accidentally slipped into feeling sorry for myself again. Just in time I remembered that I was supposed to be turning lemons into lemonade.

I put on my pyjamas and went to bed with my diet

book for company. I leafed through Dr Atkins's menu suggestions, trying to make up my mind what I could have for breakfast next morning. I decided on ham with two kinds of melted cheese. I thought two different kinds of hot melted cheese would make it seem more like a proper meal; like a Dr Atkin's version of Mario's delicious croque-monsieur. The thought made my stomach growl like a caged tiger and I longed to go downstairs and eat some melted cheese right now with thick slices of golden brown toast. *No, no toast*! I mentally slapped away the image. Melted cheese and ham would be fine. I could add a little pinch of mustard for extra interest. My mouth was watering. *Willpower*, Nat, I told myself. *You can totally do this*.

I got up and went to my basin, filled my tooth glass with water and drank it, then I refilled my glass and downed that too, even though my sisters insisted that water from an upstairs tap was bad for you. Something about dead rats in the cistern, I remembered with a shudder, but if that was true how come it was OK to use rat water to brush your teeth?

Did rats still carry plague? *Best not to think about it, Nat*, I told myself. I went back to bed refusing to dwell on what might be floating in our antiquated water cistern, and lay down in the dark with my stomach bloated and gurgling. Drinking two glasses of water hadn't stopped me feeling hungry but it had taken my mind off it a bit, not to mention wondering if I was now fatally infected with bubonic plague.

As the days went by I learned all kinds of little tricks to fool my empty stomach into believing it was full; regular sips of water, chewing gum or sucking on mints. I was still skipping lunch but I wasn't stupid. I'd never get through a workout session with slave-driver Jacek without some fuel to convert into energy, so I kept a small zip-lock bag in the pocket of my joggers filled with tiny cubes of Cheddar cheese. Every time I stopped to sip from my water bottle (Jacek was very keen on keeping us hydrated), I would furtively nibble another cube, just enough to bring up my blood sugar, then I'd go back to pounding on my treadmill to nowhere, or lifting weights or doing press-ups or whatever it was.

I also learned other tricks, sly little strategies to fool onlookers that I was eating normally. I always took my lunch box into the canteen. I even kept a couple of Doctor Karg crackers in there and a tired-looking apple, in case Billie or someone happened to look inside. I'd noticed that so long as I was careful to make it seem like I was just about to eat, opening up my lunch box, enthusiastically picking up a cracker, suddenly remembering I had promised to return a DVD to Oliver, or that I urgently needed to dash to the loo, then coming back and sinking a long drink of water because my mouth was so dry – nobody seemed to notice, and before I knew it I had survived yet another lunchtime without a single evil calorie passing my lips.

At home, on rare occasions when our family ate together I used similar distraction techniques plus a useful ruse I'd picked up from Sarah Corrie at my old school. Sarah did this thing where she was constantly moving her food around on her plate, stirring, putting some on her fork, putting her fork down to have a quick sip of water, flashing you a gorgeous smile so that she completely had you believing she was totally relishing her meal, when she was mainly skilfully hiding bits under other bits. Obviously I didn't plan to take things as far as Sarah Corrie! Sarah had a problem. I was just trying to get slim for my sister's wedding.

Jacek had told me that one technique the TV actress used to help herself lose weight before she did *Strictly* was visualisation. She kept imagining herself as slim and beautiful, totally wowing the judges in her glittering ballroom outfit. So now before I went to sleep, I deliberately pictured myself at Plum's wedding holding up my sister's train, looking poised and exquisite in my silver-grey bridesmaid's dress. Then I'd have fun imagining my stepmother's outraged astonishment. I'd be untouchable, I thought. I would have become everything Jenny had told me I could never be and she'd never be able to hurt me again. For the first time in the long-running war with my stepmother I'd have won.

Every night before I went to bed, I weighed myself on the bathroom scales to see how much weight I'd lost. At first my progress was disappointingly slow, but for the first time in my life I refused to give up. It wasn't long before I started seeing encouraging results. A combination of intense exercise and eating like a bird made the weight start to drop off. I can't describe the thrill the first time I put on a pair of my size-ten jeans and found them sagging off my bum! You'd think this discovery might have made me ease up on my dieting. But it was the opposite. The more weight I lost, the more I was determined to lose.

One morning I came downstairs to the kitchen and was surprised to find my stepmother fishing down the dogs' leads from the utility room, getting ready to take them for a walk. Betty immediately started jumping up at her excitedly. '*Sit*! You impatient little puppy!' Jenny tsked and Betty immediately sat like a good puppy, with her back straight and her nose pointing right up at Jenny, quivering with concentration as if she was about to take an extremely hard exam.

When we're in Norfolk my stepmother walks the dogs for miles through woods and across meadows. But though she's lived in London for years now, she still disliked taking them into the local parks so an old friend of Mrs Nolan's had been walking them twice a day. 'Isn't Earl coming today?' I asked her. (Jenny's dog walker really is called Earl Grey like the tea.)

I had helped myself to a banana, deliberately picking one that was going brown at one end. Not-eating in front of people was becoming an enjoyable game, almost an addiction.

'Mrs Nolan says his arthritis is playing up.' Jenny's tone suggested that Earl was doing it on purpose to irritate her. 'We're going to have to find someone else to take you walkies, aren't we, Hamish?' She ran her hands over her favourite dog's legs and haunches. This was only partly affection. Jenny was also searching for telltale hot spots where her prize male cocker might have injured himself or got the beginnings of an infection.

I peeled my banana, taking a tiny bite. 'Why have you got to find someone else?' I asked her in my most neutral voice. 'I'll walk them for you. You can pay me what you paid Earl,' I added in the same cool business-like voice, secretly thrilled at my own daring.

She gave a scornful laugh. 'How do you suppose you'll manage that and keep up with your school work?'

'Other girls do part-time jobs,' I said, thinking of Billie. 'I can get up half an hour early and walk them before I go to school, then I'll take them out after I get back from the gym.'

She gave another disbelieving laugh. 'And you really think you can be that disciplined!'

You have no idea how disciplined I can be, I thought, but I just shrugged. 'I do actually. Besides, it'll help me lose weight,' I added slyly as I carefully folded the banana skin back over my three-quarters uneaten banana.

'I must say it's a relief to see you're finally getting rid of some of that ghastly puppy fat,' she admitted reluctantly.

Those kinds of remarks used to make me shrivel in shame, but I calmly held her gaze, then in one quick movement I threw the rest of my banana in the bin. 'It was rotten,' I explained with a smile. 'Don't you just hate it when that happens?' Halfway out of the door I called, 'I haven't got time to walk the dogs now I'm afraid, but I'll definitely walk them tonight!'

I felt like a thirsty plant that had suddenly been given water. I felt sassy and confident and in control and all because I'd lost a little bit of weight!

As I hurried past a shop window on the way to school, I caught a glimpse of my reflection and for the first time ever I almost liked what I saw. *Still room for improvement though, Natalie*, I told myself. *You're not supermodel material just yet*!

I arrived at the school gates at exactly the same time as Oliver Maybury.

'Hi, Oliver,' I said with the new confidence of someone who has just got the better of her evil stepmother.

He'd been listening to his MP3 player and quickly took his ear-bud out, giving me a delighted smile. 'Oh, hi, stranger! Where have you been hiding? Louisa was just saying that you haven't been round to our house for a while.'

I shrugged. 'I know. I've just been mad busy.' I didn't think Oliver needed to know that most of my afterschool time was now taken up with my demanding exercise programme at Jacek's gym. With any luck he'd assume that any improvement in my looks had just come about naturally.

I caught myself fiddling with my hair like you sometimes see girls doing when they want a boy to notice them. Although I didn't fancy Oliver (as I am constantly explaining to my friends), I couldn't help wanting to impress him with my new improved dieting self. 'So how's it been at your house?' I asked carelessly.

Oliver rubbed his hand across his face. 'It's been quite stressful actually. We had to call the police. Eva's ex-boyfriend started stalking her.'

'Oh my God, that's terrible!' I said. 'Did the police arrest him?'

'They took him in for questioning but they had to let him go,' he said wearily.

'Seriously?' I said, startled. 'How come they didn't charge him!'

'It was just our word against his. I'm a spotty minor and Eva's excitable and foreign,' he said with a sigh. 'I don't think they took us very seriously. I bet they'd have booked him in no time if it was my mum who'd called them.'

'Is your mum still away?'

He nodded. 'She's still filming. She got her equipment back luckily. They're behind schedule now but she should be back in a couple of weeks.'

We were walking across the playground making our

way through the usual school cliques. I sailed past Tom Nash and his crew as if I didn't even know they existed, feeling a little buzz of satisfaction. I was learning that being thinner gave me a licence to behave in a totally different, even slightly outrageous, way.

I suddenly felt Oliver's eyes lingering on me. *He's noticed*, I thought. I turned to beam at him and was startled by his troubled expression. He fidgeted with the buckle on his bag. 'Um, Natalie,' he said diffidently. 'Are you sure you're OK?'

'Me?' I gave a laugh of genuine surprise. 'I've never felt so OK in my life! Why?'

'I don't know. I think maybe it's your face. It looks abnormally—'

'Looks abnormally *what*?' I almost shouted. This wasn't the kind of reaction I'd been wanting at all. What right did geeky, Pentagon-hacking Oliver have to say I was abnormal!

He looked as if he was wishing the ground would crack open and swallow him whole. 'Sorry, that was the wrong word to use. I meant it looks kind of, *sharp*. You know, *here*,' he said unhappily, pointing to his own cheek to show me what he meant.

It suddenly dawned on me what Oliver meant. 'Excuse me!' I gabbled.

I went flying in through the foyer and into the cloakroom, where I stood staring raptly at myself in the mirror. 'Oh. My. God!' I whispered.

For the first time in my life I had *cheekbones*!

I rushed to find my friends, who were just that minute walking into school, deep in conversation.

'Cheekbones!' I told them deliriously. 'I've got cheekbones. This diet is SO working!'

Ella and Billie turned with identical blank looks. 'What?'

I got the feeling I'd butted into a private talk. 'I've got cheekbones,' I repeated, feeling rather foolish now.

'Oh, right,' said Billie. 'Well, good for you, girl!'

'Yeah totally,' said Ella without enthusiasm. 'So you must be really pleased?'

'I'm over the *moon*!' I told them. 'I never knew I even had them! It's quite a surprise as you can imagine!' I gave them a big hopeful grin, waiting for my friends to say something encouraging. It's like, when I secretly know I'm getting something wrong I do that same wrong thing even more, as if somehow that will make it better. It's not a great strategy at the best of times and this didn't exactly seem to be the best of times. Ella immediately went from polite and cool to frosty ice queen. Billie just got unusually quiet. I'd done something to upset them, that was obvious. But of course being a Bonneville-St John I couldn't actually come out and ask what I'd done.

All through morning lessons I had a feeling in the pit of my stomach, like that sick feeling I get before a storm breaks.

At lunchtime, Ella stirred her tub of Greek salad around for a few minutes, carefully avoiding my eyes. Then she finally looked up and let me have it. 'You do know that Billie is DJing regularly at Mario's now?' she asked in a tight voice.

'Yes, I think it's brilliant,' I said, puzzled.

'Well, *we* all think so,' Ella said in the same unfriendly tone. 'That's why I wanted to check that you did actually know, because we can't help noticing that you're the only person in the Breakfast Club who hasn't been to see her.' She sat back in her chair, and waited to see how I'd react.

Oh, is that it. Out loud I said, 'I know that and I feel really bad about it.'

'She did *such* a cool set last Friday.' Ella was looking at me now with an openly hostile expression 'Everyone's been talking about it. I'm surprised you didn't hear.'

'Of course I heard,' I said, surprised. 'I heard you guys talking about it next morning at the Breakfast

Club and Lexie was saying how great it was.' Too late Lexie's actual words flashed back to me. 'Where were you, by the way, Natalie?' she had asked crisply. 'Wild horses keep you away again?'

I tried to remember if I'd even replied. I seemed to remember mainly being preoccupied with how to avoid actually eating the highly calorific croissants I'd ordered. Strategies that worked in the school canteen or in front of my family weren't so effective when I was sitting across from eagle-eyed Billie in one of Mario's intimate little booths. That could have been why I didn't register my friends talking excitedly about Billie's set. I was too busy watching for a moment when they were distracted so I could swiftly wrap another small chunk of apricot croissant in some paper napkin and make it disappear into my bag. I was way too savvy now to make the entire croissant disappear in one go.

Ella still had her hostile smile trained on me as she waited for me to explain myself.

'I suppose I've had quite a lot on my mind,' I said awkwardly. 'But hey, I knew you'd be brilliant, Billie,' I told her, attempting my new sassy smile. 'I'm so proud of you, I really am, and I will come, I promise, just as soon as I can.'

'So come this Friday!' Ella made it sound like a

challenge. 'Jools has given Billie VIP tickets for all her favourite people, hasn't she, Billie?'

Billie nodded then went back to silently eating her lunch.

'I can't . . . I've got to go to the gym,' I explained.

Billie was still carefully not looking at me, unlike Ella, who kept her eyes fiercely fixed on my face until I felt my new cheekbones burning with shame even though I didn't really think I'd done anything wrong. 'No way do you have to go to that gym *every* night,' she told me coldly.

I shook my head. 'No, Ella, I do. I'm working out every weekday night.'

'You seriously have to go EVERY night? You can't take an evening off?'

I took a nervous sip of water. 'No, it's a commitment that I made to myself and Plum and I'm sticking to it.'

Ella took a deep breath and I could see her trying not to lose her temper. 'Look, I know Plum's wedding is a big thing – but so are Billie's gigs a big thing! I don't believe you can't miss just *one* night.'

'Ella, believe me, if I could be in two places at once I would, but Gus is paying a *fortune* for us all to go to the gym. I can't just *not* go.'

Ella shook her head. 'This is so not you, Natalie.'

She sounded disgusted.

But it is, I thought. *It's the new me, the real me.* It seemed to me that Ella had forgotten what the Breakfast Club was supposed to be about. She seemed to think that being a 'superstar celebrity' only applied to her and the others. For some reason I was supposed to stay the same overweight, under-achieving person I'd always been. I wanted to stamp and yell like a little kid, 'That's not fair!' But if I did that, it would end in a huge blazing row and then my friends would walk away from me for ever. So instead I told them I was sorry.

'I mean it,' I said, almost in tears. 'I am really and truly sorry. If I could manage to tear myself down the middle I would! I know you think I've got a bit wrapped up in myself, Ella –'

'A *bit*!' Ella interrupted with a toss of her hair

For the first time, Billie looked up. 'Natalie just explained where she's at,' she told Ella quietly. 'She told you. She can't be in two places at once. Now drop it, OK?'

'But—' Ella started.

Billie shook her head. 'Please, Ella, just drop it. Nat's got to do what she's got to do.'

'It's not for ever,' I told her gratefully. 'After the wedding—'

'Sure, I understand.' Billie started wrapping up the remains of her lunch.

'So – um, did you hear the latest about Eva?' I asked to change the subject.

'The Mayburys' au pair?' Ella never could resist gossip. 'No, what happened?'

'Her ex-boyfriend has been stalking her. Oliver had to call the police.'

'No way!' she breathed.

I told them everything Oliver had told me. But as I chatted and laughed and gestured, I felt deeply betrayed. Weren't friends supposed to try to understand you? Because my friends didn't seem to have caught on that I wasn't just their comedy sidekick or their cheerleader, at least not any more. Like them I now had a *life*.

After school I caught the bus to the Harrow Road so Jacek could put me through another hour of torture. Some days were less of a struggle but today, halfway through my exhausting fat-busting crunches I suddenly went to pieces. 'I can't,' I said almost in tears. 'I can't do any more.'

'You think you can't,' Jacek agreed. 'But that is only in here!' He tapped his head. 'You can always do more. Always.' He went over to the water cooler and filled a plastic beaker and handed it to me with that cool glint in his eyes that wasn't quite a smile. 'I will permit my star pupil to take a break for a few moments,' he said, deadpan.

I almost choked into the glass. 'I'm seriously your star pupil?'

'If I had star pupils you would most definitely be up there,' he said gravely. 'You are making extremely good progress, Natalie. I am pleased with you. When you first started I could see you were not used to working out and I think maybe it was a little bit intimidating for you?'

'A LOT intimidating!' I admitted.

He gave me an approving nod. 'But you made up your mind to just go for it and, well, now you are seeing good results for all your hard work!'

For a moment I thought I might burst into tears. 'Thank you,' I managed huskily. 'I wish my friends thought like you.' The words just slipped out.

'Your friends don't approve of you coming to the gym?'

'I just don't think they want me to change,' I said painfully.

'Well, that is their bad luck because in this life change is inevitable,' Jacek said calmly. 'But I know how it is. Some people get twitchy if things don't stay the same.'

'That's exactly it!' I told him. 'I've always supported them. Like when Billie wanted to do the fund-raising benefit for Freya and Ella wanted to enter the fashion design competition, I was there cheering them on, you know? But now I'm doing something that's *really* important to me and they're not there for me at all!'

'Life can be tough,' Jacek agreed, 'but you are strong girl, Natalie and you will not let yourself be knocked off course by such small setbacks as this.' He took the plastic beaker out of my hand. 'Now back to work!'

On the way home on the bus I hugged Jacek's words to myself. 'You are strong girl, Natalie.' No one had ever told me I was strong before. Jacek had made me feel that he understood me, that he admired how I was sticking to my guns. Of course he didn't know that I'd virtually stopped eating. But I told myself that if he *did* know he would totally understand that it was only because I was so committed to my goal; that magical day when I'd lost so much weight that my Bridesmaidzilla nightmares would be banished for ever.

Chapter Seven

The moment they heard my key in the lock the dogs rushed to meet me, wagging their tails. Nobody else seemed to be at home. I gobbled down a Doctor Karg cracker with a piece of cheese. Then I slipped an old tennis ball in my pocket and unhooked the dogs' leads from the peg in the utility room while the dogs milled around watching my every move with hopeful expressions. 'Come on, chaps! Let's go and play in the park,' I told them.

It was a warm summer's evening but Kensington Gardens was unusually empty except for a couple of fellow dog walkers off in the distance and the occasional jogger chugging by. I let the dogs off their leads and threw the ball for them for over half an hour until they and I had had enough. Being a puppy Betty had a shockingly short concentration span. I was constantly having to race after her to stop her running up to people she had picked out to be her new best friend.

The fourth or fifth time she ran off, I picked her up under my arm and brought her back to sit beside me on the grass. The older dogs came to lie down too, panting with their tongues lolling out. I picked a small pink-edged daisy and held it out to Betty to sniff. She looked puzzled for a minute then very politely ate it. I scooped her up and hugged her. 'How cute are *you*!' I said, kissing her nose, then I had to make a huge fuss of the other dogs too because it isn't fair to have favourites.

The sky over the park was streaked shiny yellow-gold with sunset and it suddenly seemed like everything had brighter colours than usual. A pigeon zipped past over my head with a whir of wings and its feathers seemed more sharply feathery than they normally would, if that makes sense? Everything seemed even *more* like itself, sharper, brighter, shinier and in Betty's case, even cuter! It was almost like being on drugs, not that I'd taken drugs but it's the kind of feeling drug-takers describe. I'd had a few of these crystal clear moments lately. They seemed to go along with feeling fiercely hungry. It was like I'd lost – not just weight – but some crucial layer between me and the universe. It was a strangely beautiful but also scary feeling, as if I was just about to step off some kind of edge.

On the way home my mobile started to ring. It was Lexie. 'Hi, Lexie! What a nice surprise!' I said genuinely happy to hear from my super-busy friend. 'I've just been in the park with the dogs. It's *such* a lovely evening, isn't it?'

'Lovely for you maybe,' Lexie said tersely.

It turned out she hadn't phoned for a friendly catch-up or to listen to me babble about how beautiful the park had looked at sunset. She wanted to tear me off a strip for upsetting Billie.

'When? *When* did I upset her?' I was genuinely confused.

'I'll give you a list, shall I?' she said to my dismay. 'You upset her the first time because you obviously couldn't be bothered to come to her gig and didn't even have the decency to tell her why. Then you upset her again at Mario's on Saturday when you acted like you couldn't care less how her set had gone down. Then you upset her all over *again* today at school when Ella told you that Jools had given Billie VIP tickets for everyone in the Breakfast Club and you just dissed the whole thing!'

'Billie wasn't upset though!' I said, astonished. 'It was just a misunderstanding and anyway we totally made it up. And I didn't "diss" anything for your information. I just can't manage to be in two places at once.'

'Nat, *trust* me, Billie was upset. Ella said she was in floods, she just didn't let on to you. I want to know what you're planning to do about it?'

I could feel myself starting to tremble, like Betty when we tell her she's been a bad puppy. My crystal clear moment in the park already seemed like a distant memory. 'But I *told* her I had to go to the gym.' My throat ached as if I was going to cry. 'Billie said she understood. She told Ella to get off my case.'

'Because she still has some pride,' Lexie said angrily. 'Because she could see you care more about your pointless weight-loss programme than you care about her, and Billie didn't want to humiliate herself any more than you had already.'

I couldn't take it in. I couldn't believe Lexie was even saying these things. How long had my friends been feeling this way, talking about me behind my back? And how come I hadn't known about it until now? 'I thought you'd understand.' I was almost whispering into my mobile.

'What's to understand?' Lexie demanded. 'It's not rocket science, Nat! One of our friends needed your support!'

'Oh, so *I* don't need support, is that it!' I burst out.

'What exactly do you need support with?' she asked icily.

'Why you are all *being* like this?' My voice cracked. 'You have to know how hard this has been for me! You know what I'm like. You know what my family is like.'

'I'm lost,' Lexie said coldly. 'What are we talking about now?'

'*Me*, Lexie! Remember, I'm supposed to be getting in shape for my sister's wedding?' I could feel my entire body vibrating with the sheer effort of having this conversation in the middle of a busy London street.

'And that's it, is it?' Lexie's voice was scathing. 'God, Nat, when are you going to get a *life*!'

'That's exactly what I'm *trying* to do if you'd all just get off my case!' I yelled. 'You're the one who said I should work out. "Oh, Nat, *everybody* can benefit from a workout". Those were your actual words, Lexie, don't deny it! And now that I'm actually *doing* it everybody's giving me a hard time!'

The dogs were staring at me in dismay, obviously wondering why I was yelling to myself in the middle of the street. Betty wagged her tail, doing her foolish doggie grin like she was saying, 'Is it something I've done?'

'Oh, so now it's *my* fault,' said Lexie in the same cold voice.

'No! I just—' *Oh, what's the point!* I thought despairingly, Lexie and the others had obviously made up their minds I was a vain, selfish cow and nothing I could say would make any difference.

'I don't know what planet you're on these days . . .' Lexie started.

I couldn't stand to listen to any more. I ended the call mid-sentence and ran home with the dogs, half blinded by my tears.

That evening in my room when I'd had a chance to cool down I re-ran Lexie's phone call in my mind and something cold and clammy crept into the pit of my stomach and refused to go away.

I remembered how I'd insisted that Billie wasn't upset, having based this on the evidence that my friend never actually came out and *told* me she was upset. I pictured Billie silently chewing her lunch looking as if every mouthful tasted like ashes, a detail I'd managed to overlook when it was actually happening. There had been other little details that had passed me by. Like the way Billie wasn't able to bring herself to look at me, and the way she was possibly (God, this was horrible) trying really hard not to cry.

I felt so bad I had to get up and pace. This meant opening my door and going out on to the landing between the attics. My room is much too small for pacing.

I should have explained, I thought guiltily. *I shouldn't have just not turned up.* This probably sounds dumb, but I genuinely hadn't thought I'd be missed. Ella and the others were going and a bunch of people from school. Jools and her fiancé Louis would be there and Dino and his crew and loads of Billie's mates from Ladbroke Grove. Why would she need me?

Billie is always telling me off for assuming my friends can read my mind. Was that what I'd done? Had I expected them to be mind-readers, to understand that I still really cared about them despite the fact that I hadn't shown up to my best friend's first ever public outing as a professional DJ?

I don't know what planet you're on.

I wasn't sure I did either. I'd been so sure I was doing the right thing, working flat-out to become the superstar celebrity Natalie. But how could it be the right thing if people were getting hurt?

As it turned out I wasn't the only one doing some soul searching. When I checked my phone before I went to sleep, in the unlikely event that one of my friends had left a message, there was a text from Lexie to say she was sorry for being such a stroppy moo. She knew she'd come on a bit strong. It had been a horrible day for reasons she wouldn't go into now, but she didn't have to take it out on me.

I cried tears of relief all over Betty.

At school next day I went straight up to Billie and begged her to forgive me. I told her that I'd been going through a tough time but I was fine now and I honestly hadn't thought she'd miss me at the gig. She immediately threw her arms around me and we both had a little cry. 'You're mad, Natalie!' she said, wiping her eyes. 'Why wouldn't I miss one of my best friends?'

'Hey, I know that *now*!' I did a watery giggle. 'Mind you I did have to stay up half the night to figure it out!' I admitted ruefully.

'What *are* we going to do with you, girl?' Billie said with affection.

I didn't say this to Billie or I might have burst out crying all over again, but even now after all we've been through together, I am still sometimes astonished to have found such great friends. It's almost like, somewhere inside, I still can't quite believe it.

I floated through the next few hours in a fuzzy pink

cloud. My friends liked me again. Everything was going to be OK.

And everything kept on being totally OK until midway through the afternoon when we went to change for PE. As I took off my shirt I caught my friends looking at me with horrified expressions. Ella quickly turned away like she couldn't bear to look.

'What?' I said, alarmed. 'What's wrong?'

'Girl, I can see your bones,' Billie said bluntly. 'You are painfully thin. This dieting business has got *way* out of hand. You need to stop this foolishness right now, before you do some real harm to yourself.'

That's all it took to send my fuzzy pink cloud crashing to earth. Billie was still looking me up and down in a way that made me want to grab my towel and cover myself up, but I didn't seem able to move. My legs started to tremble. I felt unbelievably exposed, guilty and scared. Avoiding my friends' anxious looks, I quickly finished changing and scurried to join the other girls in the gym.

After PE, I went to get changed in the loos away from the worried eyes of my friends. I looked down at myself, replaying my friends' reactions. Had I really got so disturbingly thin?

I realised I was shaking again. All kinds of things

made me shaky these days. It was one of the side effects of cutting down on my calorie intake; along with waking up with a disgusting bad taste in my mouth, which made me worried that my breath smelled.

What planet are you on? I'd been on Planet Weight Loss, I thought, swallowing. Maybe my friends were right, maybe I'd gone too far? I remembered that feeling of crystal clarity in the park. How it felt so beautiful yet also like I was about to step over some kind of dangerous edge. I hadn't stepped over it though – not yet. I could still change back to the old Nat. All I had to do was start eating again.

I could start today, I thought. I could invite my friends to go with me to the Hummingbird Bakery after school as my treat. We'd eat coffee and maple syrup cupcakes with all the designer mummies! I could already smell the divine freshly baked cupcake smell that always fills the Hummingbird Bakery. I could feel the meltingly soft crumbs in my mouth, the sweetness of the maple syrup and the tiny kick of caffeine. I was almost drooling at the thought.

I waited until we were coming out of school to issue my invitation. I had actually drawn a breath to say those exact words. But just then Eddie Jones, Ella's not-so-secret admirer, went past and he and

Ella had one of their flirty exchanges. It was only a few seconds before Ella turned back to me and Billie, but by that time someone else had come strolling past us with his crew.

My good intentions died on my lips as Tom Nash turned his head, bad boy hair falling across his forehead, to give me the cool stare that made me go weak at the knees. 'Hi, Natalie. Might see you tomorrow, yeah?' he said smoothly then strolled on by.

Billie had no time for Tom Nash and completely ignored his interruption. 'Sorry, Nat, were you going to say something?' she asked.

My heart was still madly looping the loop. I quickly shook my head.

It was like a sign from above. I had finally become visible to Tom Nash. No way was I giving up my diet now!

When I got home our sitting room was filled with creamy fabric.

I'd forgotten that today was the day Plum's dressmaker was bringing our calico *toiles*, cheap cotton versions of our wedding finery to try on for fit and size. Iris had already made Nelly try on her *toile*. Plum was going to go up to her room with Iris to have her dress fitted in private. Plum planned to keep her dress a secret from everyone until her wedding day.

I watched Iris deftly taking in the bodice seam of Matilda's outfit. With her fists tightly clenched, my little cousin was forcing herself to stand still, though she flinched dramatically every time Iris approached her with a pin. I gave her a wave. 'Hi, Matilda?'

She stared at me confused as if she wasn't completely sure who I was. 'Hello,' she said in a polite but worried voice, then her expression cleared and she gave a nervous giggle. 'Sorry! For a minute I didn't think you were my Natalie!'

'Of course I'm still your Natalie. Who else would I be!'

Matilda still looked spooked. 'I didn't really know. You sound like my Natalie, but you haven't got her face.'

When it was my turn to try on my *toile*, Iris gave me an astonished glance, held up my outfit and said, bewildered, 'I don't know what I was thinking when I took down your measurements, Natalie! Can you just put it on for me then I can pin it to see exactly where I need to take it in.'

I ran off to change then came back in self-consciously clutching my gaping bodice to my chest.

'Oh, quickly, sweetie, come here!' Iris hastily rescued my modesty with a few well-placed pins. 'I can't believe I got it so wrong. This dress is totally drowning you!'

'I've lost a little bit of weight,' I confessed, flushing.

'Gus is paying for us all to work with a personal trainer,' Plum explained proudly. 'You know at that new gym on the Harrow Road? This guy is AMAZING. He reckons he can get anyone to drop two dress sizes.'

'I'd say Natalie's done that easily,' Iris said still busy pinning.

'You really think I'm a size six?' I gasped.

Inside I was going 'Whoo-whee!' Size six was like Willy Wonka's Golden Ticket, the impossible dream that you never really thought would come true!

'I'd say so, definitely.' I noticed that Iris didn't seem as enthusiastic about this news as my sister Plum, who actually clapped. 'Didn't I tell you Jacek would make you look exquisite!' she said, beaming at me.

Relief flashed through me. Plum wouldn't say I was 'exquisite', would she? Not if I was as 'painfully thin' as Billie said.

Nellie was engrossed in texting someone, smiling secretively to herself and didn't seem to notice she'd acquired a new willowy size-six sister. Although I really hated myself for this, I couldn't help turning to Jenny.

Maybe now I had finally won her seal of approval?

My stepmother's lips tightened. 'She'd look a lot better if she'd learn to stand up straight,' she commented to Plum as if I wasn't there. 'Stop that *awful* slouching, Natalie, and put your shoulders back for *goodness'* sake!'

Purely out of habit I obeyed her, but as I did it I had my own private rebellion. I mentally summoned up a picture of Tom Nash as he turned to look at me outside the school gates. *See you tomorrow, Natalie*. He'd made it sound like a promise.

I felt my stepmother's eyes follow me coldly as I sped off to get my gym things for my after-school work-out. You'd think I'd have figured out by now that nothing I could do would make my stepmother love or even *like* me. So it was humiliating to realise that some part of me had obviously kept a spark of hope alight; *Now* she'll love me, now she's seen how hard I've tried, how thin I'm looking, now I've lost all that shameful disgusting *weight*.

This afternoon I finally understood that this would never change. But something else *was* changing. Jenny knew she was losing her grip over me. I could see it in her eyes – and I'd done it by beating her at her own game! I had actually *out-dieted* my stepmother! *Size six*! I thought exultantly. I'd done it! I'd won the golden ticket to my Happy Ever After, where sexy boys like Tom Nash noticed me – and there was nothing she could do about it!

I was on a bus halfway up the Harrow Road, stuck in heavy traffic when my mobile went. Either Ella was going down with a cold or she'd been crying. 'I just wanted to ask you if you had any idea where I might have left my designs?'

'You mean for the competition?'

'Yeah, at least half of them are missing from my portfolio. I've looked everywhere at home. I rang the school and actually spoke to Mrs Spelling and she says I didn't leave them behind in the art room.'

'No, sorry, Ella, I haven't seen them.' I was standing up, trying to see if the traffic had started to move up ahead.

'I just wish I could remember when I last saw them.' Ella sounded slightly hysterical. 'I mean, they can't just have *disappeared*, can they? I just don't know what I'll do if I can't find them.'

'You didn't make copies?'

'No, it never occurred to me I'd need to. I'm so dumb!' She gave a teary laugh. 'I worked so hard on those drawings. I don't think I've ever worked so hard at anything ever.'

'You'll find them!' I told her, and I genuinely hoped she did, but I was inwardly panicking about being late for my appointment at the gym. Maybe I should jump off and go the rest of the way on foot?

'I really hope so,' Ella said unhappily.

I decided the bus wasn't going anywhere. 'Sorry, Ells, I've got to run. I really hope your drawings turn up.' I scrambled down from the top deck, jumped off the bus and went racing through traffic fumes towards Jacek.

Next day Ella's designs still hadn't shown up. She had been hoping against hope that someone might have found them and handed them in, but when she went to ask the school secretary before lunch nobody had.

In the canteen Billie comforted her as she fought back her tears. I was genuinely sorry for Ella but I was also completely distracted because Tom Nash had deliberately come to sit next to me at our table. He kept accidentally on purpose touching his leg against mine, making the kind of teasing comments boys make to girls they fancy. I half wanted to flirt back but I was feeling increasingly weird. The sunlight coming through the huge windows was too bright, and the noises of cutlery and people's voices seemed to be booming around inside my head so there was no room for anything else.

It was a relief when we eventually escaped from the noise and food smells of the dinner hall. Ella dramatically clutched at my arm. 'Did you hear him?' she said in a choked voice.

'Hear who?' I asked vaguely, wishing the booming sounds would stop.

'Joe Grupetta! Did you really not hear him running his mouth about how brilliant he is?'

'I think Nat had other things on her mind,' Billie said tactfully.

We hurried down the corridor towards our favourite lesson of the week, double drama with Mr Berolli. Tamsin must have come running after us because she was suddenly right up in my face.

As well as being a wannabe Alpha, Tamsin carried a not so secret crush for Oliver Maybury. 'I saw you snuggling up to Tom Nash just now,' she hissed. 'Well, now you've finally got Tom to fancy you maybe you'll let Oliver out of your clutches, and give someone *else* a chance!' Having delivered her message she fled into the girls' toilets.

I just stood in the middle of the corridor not quite understanding what had just happened. Billie and Ella quickly put their arms around me.

'You OK?' Billie asked.

I nodded shakily. 'I'm fine. God, what *is* her problem?'

'Her problem is she's Tamsin,' Billie said, shaking her head. 'I don't think it's much fun being Tamsin.'

'Doesn't look like it,' I said with difficulty. My voice seemed to be coming from somewhere outside myself.

Ella suddenly seemed to shake off her depression. 'I've decided what I'm going to do,' she announced. 'Don't tell anyone but I'm going to take tomorrow off so I can redo my designs! I mean, if I want to be a fashion designer, I've got to learn to overcome these kinds of little setbacks, right?' She said it was hearing Joe Grupetta boasting that did it. It made her that much more determined to win the competition!'

'Good for you, girl,' said Billie.

'Yes, good for you,' I echoed, making a tremendous effort to reach my friends through the roaring in my head. The back of my neck was suddenly wet with sweat. 'I'm just going to get a drink of water,' I said desperately. Then the world went black and one of my more extreme fantasies came true in the worst way as I crumpled into a dead faint at the feet of Mr Berolli.

Chapter Eight

'What a lovely man,' Mrs Nolan kept exclaiming all the way home. 'What a lovely, *lovely* man.' I sat in the passenger seat of her tiny blue Fiat, leaning weakly against the window, thinking that one day when I had the money I would have to pay a hypnotist to liberate my lost memories of being carried along the corridor to the medical room in Mr Berolli's arms.

Billie and Ella had rushed after him and were there with me in the medical room when I came round. They stayed with me until Mrs Nolan came to take me home. That's how I learned about Mr Berolli picking me up off the floor.

I was mortified. 'I'll never be able to face him again,' I told my friends as I lay woozily on the medical room's hard metal bed.

'Hey, you looked good together, girl,' Billie joked.

'Mr Berolli was striding along all masterful with you in his arms, telling everyone to get out of his way. You looked like a swooning Victorian heroine, white as chalk, with your beautiful curly hair all hanging down and your limp little hands dangling!'

'It was actually quite cool!' Ella agreed.

'Yeah, Nat, it's just a real shame you missed it!' My friends had been kidding around as if nothing had happened but anyone could see they were shaken up. I'd secretly waited for them to say something about my dieting but neither of them had.

I was sitting at the kitchen table sipping a reviving hot cup of tea when Jenny walked in. She'd been out shopping without her mobile when the school phoned. That's why Mrs Nolan had to come and fetch me.

'Well, *you* look like a bit of a wreck, Natalie,' my stepmother said sharply as she bent down to pet Betty's mother Tulip. 'Not still having your funny turns are you?' 'Funny turns' is what my stepmother always called my boarding school panic attacks.

Mrs Nolan was stacking the dishwasher and suddenly started slamming plates and cutlery into their slots as if she was imagining flinging them at Jenny's head. 'Panic attacks, what piffle! This girl has been starving herself right in front of your eyes and it's beyond my understanding how you keep refusing to see it!'

'Oh, don't be so *dramatic*, she's not "starving"!' Jenny just sounded bored. 'It's probably just her hormones kicking in. I was constantly fainting when I was her age.'

'I think I might go up to my room,' I said feebly, not feeling up to this confrontation.

I went back to bed and slept and woke and slept some more. Mrs Nolan woke me up once coming into my room before she left off work for the day. She'd brought a bowl of home-made soup to build up my strength. I polished off the soup and the thinly buttered toast she brought to accompany it then I had another little doze until Ella rang me on my mobile.

'How's you, babe?' she asked.' Any better?'

'Not sure,' I said groggily. 'I've mostly been sleeping since I got home.

'Are you awake enough to talk?'

'I think so.' I cautiously dragged myself into a sitting position and was relieved that at least everything had stopped spinning.

'I walked home with Oliver,' Ella said. 'I didn't realise he lives just round the corner from me'

'Yes I know.'

'We talked a bit about you.' Ella's tone suddenly

changed. 'Nat, even Oliver says you haven't been yourself and he's a *boy*.'

'What does that even *mean*? You're not yourself?' I would have yelled the question at her but I didn't have the energy. 'Exactly which self do you think is my "real" self? I suppose you think it's the posh girl who can't get a boyfriend because she's too *fat*!'

Ella went quiet for a moment then she said sharply, 'I hate when you talk about yourself like that. We all do.'

'And you also hate when I'm thin and pretty and boys fancy me,' I snapped. 'It seems to me that I can't win with you guys these days.'

'That's not fair, and you know it,' Ella said after another pause. 'Look, let's not fight on the phone. I really wanted to run something by you.'

'Oh, OK . . . !' I was secretly surprised that Ella still thought I was capable of giving good advice.

'You know I ran into Oliver? Well, we didn't just talk about you, OK? I told him about losing my designs and he is almost sure that Joe stole them. He heard him saying something to Marie Louise.

I gasped. 'That's terrible. How can he expect to get away with that?'

'Very easily!' she said bitterly. 'You know what Joe's

like. He's got that smooth way with him that makes people believe in him. And if he's able to convince the judges my designs are his, I can't prove he's lying.'

I'd been living inside my own little bubble for weeks now but Ella's distress suddenly got through in the most shocking way. 'Ella, that's *terrible*! What are you going to do?'

'The only thing I can think of is if I come up with a set of totally different, even better designs.'

'But that means you'll be competing against yourself!' I pointed out. 'You're already worn out from doing the original designs. Ella. Designing another set of uniforms is going to *really* take it out of you. If you're not careful Mr Berolli will be carrying *you* off to the medical room!' I added, only half joking.

'I don't really have a choice, Nat. If I just lie down and take it, he's won, hasn't he?'

'I guess,' I said doubtfully.

'I can't let having my designs stolen stop me entering the competition.'

'But do you think you can do it?'

'I won't know, will I, until I try?'

'True,' I agreed. 'But you know what, Ella, if anybody can pull it off, it's you. I think you're really brave to just pick yourself up and try again.'

'Thank you,' Ella said seriously. 'Thanks, Nat. That really means a lot.'

We chatted for a while then she said, 'You going back to school tomorrow?'

'Mrs Nolan says not,' I told her. 'She thinks I need to rest up.'

'Mrs Nolan's got the right idea,' said Ella. 'You should maybe listen to her more often?' It was the closest she'd come to scolding me since my big faint. Maybe she thought that was punishment enough? I thought hopefully.

I stayed home for another day, letting Mrs Nolan feed me up with bowls of her home-made chicken and watercress soup. 'There's almost no calories in it, Natalie!' she insisted, though I'm not sure if Mrs Nolan would recognise a calorie if it waved to her in the street. 'But the watercress is very strengthening for your blood. There's a ton of iron in watercress!'

Whether it was all the sleep or Mrs Nolan's watercress I don't know, but I felt much better when I got up to go to school next day.

'Oh, *yay*!' Billie said when she saw me and a tired, pale Ella hurrying towards her across the playground. She flung her arms around us both. 'I so missed you guys! I was beginning to feel like Billie No-mates!' She took a step back so she could examine me and Ella at arm's length. 'Hmm. You look better than last time I saw you, Ms Bonneville-St John, but Ms Swanson here looks like horse poo!'

'I know!' said Ella, grinning. 'But I don't care because I have come up with a whole new batch of designs!'

Billie and I both stared at her, amazed.

'Oh my God, Ella, I don't believe you actually did it!' Billie said.

'I had to stay up practically all night but they're finished!' Ella patted her portfolio. 'Fancy coming with me to hand them in to Mrs Spelling? After what happened last time I feel like I need my crew around me for security, know what I'm saying!'

'Ooh, listen to you, rude girl!' said Billie, laughing. 'You're talking like a Ladbroke Grove girl now!'

We all marched along the corridor to the art room and delivered Ella's designs safely into the hands of Mrs Spelling. Ella said she'd never felt so shattered but she was really proud of herself for hanging on in.

'Who knew I had so much willpower?' she said.

I felt like I was well-qualified to join in this conversation. 'I didn't used to get willpower either,' I said earnestly. 'Then I got the message like you, Ella. I never stuck with a diet before, but now I remind myself to stay focused on my desired goal like Jacek says.'

I realised that my friends were looking at me with troubled expressions.

'You really think you and Ella are talking about the same thing, don't you?' Billie said almost pityingly.

'Aren't we?'

She shook her head. 'Look, Nat, willpower is fine if you're using it to achieve something like, *solid*.'

'Solid?' I said. 'What does that mean, solid?'

'Something *real*, Natalie! Getting up an hour early to skate, or staying up to write a song, or redo designs. But using willpower to starve your body of the food it needs to be healthy – how is that an achievement?'

'I have done something real,' I blustered, hoping I wouldn't burst into tears. 'I've *really* been working out at the gym. I've kept going even though every bone and every muscle in my body was *really* killing me! I've *really* dropped two whole dress sizes. How is all that not real?'

'It's *why* you're doing it!' Billie said, shaking her head. 'Who is it you're trying to impress? Plum and Nellie? Your stepmother? Random boys? Do you even *know*?'

I refused to answer her. I just looked away so they wouldn't see my eyes well up. If I'd thought my friends were going to ease up on me because of my fainting fit, I was wrong. And it turned out they hadn't finished with me yet.

At lunchtime, I was playing my usual games, sipping water, remembering something I'd left in my locker, opening my lunch box, letting my friends see me breaking off a miniscule corner of a Doctor Karg cracker, but going into fits of laughter just as I was going to eat it and insisting on telling them my funny story. A part of me was thinking that this was a really tiring way to live, like going round endlessly in a hamster wheel. But how could I give up now that I knew it was finally working?

Then I felt a chill settle over our table and noticed that neither Ella or Billie were even listening to my story. Actually I got the impression they were basically waiting for me to shut up.

'What?' I said nervously.

They exchanged glances and it seemed like Ella got the short straw because she told Billie quietly, 'OK, I'll tell her.' She took a deep breath. 'Nat, we've been trying to make up our minds what to do about you.'

I opened my mouth outraged but Billie said, 'Hear her out, Nat.'

'We all love you, Nat. You know that. But we've had

to face the fact that however much we care, we're probably not the right people for you to talk to about your . . . eating problem.'

'Right,' I said coldly, fighting a desperate urge to run.

Ella swallowed. 'For one thing we know you too well but most of all we're girls and girls always think other girls are jealous of each other being skinny.' Ella had to stop for another deep breath. 'But, we thought you might agree to talk to Oliver,' she said in a rush.

There were so many different emotions fighting inside my body I could hardly speak. 'Talk to Oliver!' I managed at last. 'Are you insane? I'm not talking to Oliver Maybury about my private business!'

'Lexie said you'd say that,' said Ella.

'*Lexie's* in on this, too!' I said in disbelief.

'Of course; we're your friends,' Ella said quietly. 'We can't stand by and just watch you destroy yourself.'

'Oh, don't be so dramatic!' I told her then broke into goose-bumps as I remembered my stepmother mocking Mrs Nolan in exactly those words.

Ella didn't react, just stubbornly went on with her speech. 'So here's the deal we all came up with, Natalie. Either you talk to Oliver or we'll make an appointment with the school counsellor.'

I actually jumped up out of my seat. 'You are kidding!'

'Do we look like we're kidding?' Billie asked soberly. 'Oliver is your friend. He's worried sick about you. Please, Natalie, talk to him before you get seriously anorexic.'

I had a sick whirling sensation in my gut. I couldn't believe that Billie had just used *that* word about *me*. I sat back down on my chair but only because there didn't seem to be anywhere else to go 'I'm *not* "anorexic",' I hissed, terrified that someone would hear this humiliating conversation. 'I've *seen* anorexics and they don't look *anything* like me. All I'm doing is losing weight for my sister's wedding. How many more times have I got to explain?'

'That's the deal, Nat,' Ella said coolly as if I hadn't spoken.

I felt totally trapped. I thought I'd rather die than go to the school counsellor. They'd want to speak to my dad and Jenny. Wouldn't Jenny just love that? Nutty Natalie screws up once again.

'It's your call,' Billie said quietly.

'Fine!' I blazed at her. 'I'll talk to him! Humiliate me in front of my friend, why don't you!'

Ella just nodded. 'Oliver said he'll wait for you after

school.' She looked totally wiped now as if this conversation had taken what was left of her energy.

I spent the afternoon flipping between self-pity and squirming shame and back again. The thought of talking to Oliver about what Billie and Ella offensively called my 'eating problem', made me want to run and just keep running. It was only the threat of the counsellor that was making me hold to my promise. Billie and Ella had got me cornered and they knew it.

At afternoon break I told them I needed time to think about what I was going to say to Oliver and went for a wander around the playground. Really I just wanted to be away from the anxious expressions of my friends; my so-called friends, I thought bitterly.

I was mooching along past the gym when a cool voice said, 'Hi.' It was Tom Nash managing to look like he just happened to be cruising in the same direction. 'You're looking very serious today,' he said in a teasing voice.

'Yeah?' I said carelessly. 'Maybe I'm *feeling* serious, ever think of that?'

Tom did his husky laugh that I had so often heard directed at other, thinner, prettier girls. 'Not you, Natalie. You're a fun girl! You just need the right person to have fun with.'

'Is that right?' I felt myself flushing as it dawned on me that I was flirting; proper shameless flirting. I had heard other girls talking to boys in exactly the same bored tone so you'd swear they had no interest in the boy whatsoever. Yet somehow they'd keep finding another needling little thing to say to keep the flirting going. 'What if I don't know anyone fun though?' I asked, looking up under my lashes.

He shrugged. 'I might know someone.' He held my gaze for a moment, doing his trademark bad boy stare, then he casually pushed his hair out of his eyes and my knees totally went to jelly.

'How well do you know him though?' I asked, reminding myself to breathe.

'Pretty well,' he said, nodding. 'In fact I'd say we're quite close.'

We seemed to be standing quite a bit nearer to each other suddenly without either of us actually moving.

'We're near neighbours, did you know that?' he asked abruptly.

'You and your *friend*?' I said flippantly though we both knew that wasn't what he meant.

'Me and you,' he said. 'I thought we could walk home together one time. Maybe tonight?'

I shrugged. 'OK.'

'Later then,' he said, lifting a hand in a gesture that was almost too casual to be a wave.

'All right,' I said as if I didn't much care.

And Tom Nash went cruising off to wherever he'd been heading before he stopped to talk to me.

What a difference five minutes makes! Just five little minutes and I'd gone from the pit of shame to sexy minx!

'The fresh air must have done you good, girl,' Billie said approvingly as I slid into my usual seat between her and Ella. You've got some roses in your cheeks again.'

Miss Tempest the history teacher walked in and instead of launching straight into the Industrial Revolution, she started writing on the whiteboard in her neat teacher's writing. *What can we learn from history?*

'Well, if *you* don't know, miss!' someone quipped.

Miss Tempest just ignored him. 'Does anyone want to tell me?' she asked the class. 'Why is it so so crucially important for us to understand our history.'

Oliver put up his hand. 'So we don't keep repeating the same mistakes?'

Oliver! A flash of pure horror went through me. I had totally erased my promise to my friends from my memory.

There was no way I could go back on it. I'd seen the steely glint in Ella and Billie's eyes and didn't doubt that they'd carry out their threat to drag me off to the counsellor. On the other hand I knew enough about Tom Nash not to risk standing him up on our first – not *date* exactly, but as good as. Tom had crowds of girls swooning after him. This was an offer that might never come my way again.

Think, Natalie, I told myself desperately. To my relief I saw a way that I could salvage my almost date. I'd simply rush to find Tom at the end of school, explain that I had something tedious to get out of the way then I'd catch him up by the school gate.

I have to say Tom didn't look too thrilled at the prospect of hanging about waiting for me, but after scowling moodily into the distance for a while (he really did look spookily like Judd Nelson!) he reluctantly agreed.

'Don't be too long though!' he called as I flew off to my dreaded appointment with Oliver.

He was waiting in the foyer. When he saw me he hurried anxiously towards me as if he thought I might somehow fail to see a tall, lanky boy with curly hair. 'Natalie?'

'Yes, all *right*,' I snapped. At that moment the sight

of Oliver Maybury irritated me more than I could bear. I hated that my friends had put me in this horribly embarrassing situation and I really hated that sweet-natured Oliver, with his kind, worried eyes, was preventing me from flying straight out of school into the arms of Tom Nash.

'Well, go on,' I challenged him. 'Let's get it over with.'

'I knew you'd be like this,' he muttered half to himself, then he stared helplessly down at his trainers, as if he had no clue what to say next.

'Look, I have actually got a *life?*' I said spitefully. I swear that until that moment I honestly hadn't planned to mention Tom or our date that wasn't quite a date. But something about Oliver and his constant *niceness* made me want to stick the knife right in, and show Oliver Maybury once and for all that I had moved way beyond our cosy evenings sharing pizza and watching lame movies. I was a slim sassy minx who could have any boy she liked. Before I knew it I heard myself brag, 'If you don't mind, Tom Nash is waiting for me to walk home with him, so if you were planning to give me a lecture, don't!'

Oliver's expression didn't change but I knew my little poison dart had gone home because I felt it go deep into what was left of my heart. He just took it, that's the kind of annoying boy Oliver was. He didn't try to hurt me back or ask me why I was being such a cow. He just slowly absorbed this new piece of information. 'I see,' he said at last. 'I didn't realise that you and Tom—'

'Why don't I make it easy for you?' I interrupted. 'I'll give you your lines. You: "Natalie, have you got an eating disorder?" Me: "No. Oliver, I have *not* got an eating disorder. I just wanted to drop a couple of kilos so I can look halfway decent in my bridesmaid's outfit on my sister's Very Important Day." You: "Oops. Feeling like a real dickhead now! That'll teach me not to jump to conclusions. But don't worry, that's absolutely the last time I'll try to interfere with your life." Me: "Apology accepted, dickhead!" There! Now we can both go home!'

'No,' he said flatly. 'You can't just blag your way out of this, Natalie. You've got to actually listen to what I've got to say.'

Looking increasingly stern, Oliver worked his way through his speech while I stood looking at my fingernails, smiling coldly to myself, making it offensively clear that I wasn't listening to a single word.

When he'd finally got to the end, I said. 'Finished?

Well, you've done your duty, Oliver, now if you don't mind I've got to run.'

With my heart beating in my throat, I hurried off to meet Tom. I hadn't been sure he'd wait for me, but amazingly he was still there lounging against a wall talking to a mate on his mobile.

As Tom and I set off through the streets of Notting Hill, I told myself over and over how thrilled I was to finally have this gorgeous moody boy all to myself. But all I could see was Oliver's solemn expression turn to hurt, and me smirking and looking down at my nails as if I was in training to be my own stepmother.

After I'd said goodbye to Tom, I collected my gym things and went off to the Harrow Road, then I came home and walked the dogs. For the first time when I threw her the ball, Betty very proudly brought it back. I petted her and told her she was a clever girl but it felt like I was doing everything through a hot fog of misery.

What is wrong with you Natalie? I asked myself miserably. I'd finally got what I wanted. Out of all the girls in our school, Tom Nash had picked *me*. He had taken time out of his busy flirting schedule to flirt with *me*. On the way home his shoulder had deliberately touched mine several times. There had been a moment when I thought he was going to kiss me. I mean, *Tom Nash*! I should be walking on air!

I was the opposite of walking on air. I seemed to have fallen into a pit of self-loathing. I kept telling myself angrily that it was all Oliver's fault for meddling but I couldn't seem to make my heart believe it.

I know something that will make you feel better, I thought, perking up.

I took my sassy red tea dress off my clothes rail and quickly slipped it on, then I ran downstairs in my bare feet to admire my new boy-attracting minxy self in Plum's mirror. But when I actually came face to face with my reflection I had to swallow hard as for the first time I saw just how much weight I'd lost.

The clingy fabric that used to mould itself around my curves now hung off me like a flowery tent. And though I was nowhere near as thin as she had been, just for a moment the eyes looking back at me from the mirror were Sarah Corrie's scared bush baby eyes.

Chapter Nine

For the past two months the only dates in my diary were gym, gym, gym, gym, gym; and obviously the Breakfast Club. I'd got so into my new routine that I somehow forgot that each day was taking us one day nearer to my sister's actual wedding. One evening I got back from the gym to find Nellie and Plum sitting at the kitchen table with Diet Cokes, arguing about Plum's hen night.

'You've got to have one, hasn't she, Nat?' Nellie appealed to me.

Plum looked exasperated. 'Nellie, how many *times* do I have to tell you? If I had *wanted* a hen thing, I'd have organised a proper hen weekend. We could all have gone off to Seville or somewhere and taken tango lessons or whatever people do!'

'Why didn't you?' Nellie said. 'It would have been

fun!'

Plum started listing the reasons on her fingers. 'One. Because hen nights are just so tacky. Two. Because hen nights are about a last mad night of freedom and I don't feel like that about Gus. I can't wait to be married to him.'

Nellie blinked at her. 'Wow, you really mean it, don't you?'

'Of course I mean it,' Plum said, startled. 'I'm marrying him, aren't I? Don't you feel like that about Rupert?'

'You've only given us two reasons, hasn't she, Natalie?' Nellie said.

'Hey, leave me out of it,' I said, getting a low-calorie lemonade out of the fridge.

'So far we've had hen nights are tacky, you don't want a last night of freedom because you and Gus are so in lurve,' Nellie reeled off. 'So what's reason Number Three?'

Plum sighed. 'Because Gus and I talked about it and we agreed that neither of us wants the stag-night, hen-night thing. We just want to get married and go off to Singapore and start our new life. You can understand that, can't you?'

'Oh.' Nellie suddenly got very busy looking for

something in her new Orla Keily bag. Whatever she was looking for mustn't have been there because after a while she closed her bag and gave Plum a warm smile. 'Obviously you're totally set against having a hen night, but what if I booked us into the Mandarin Oriental spa for an afternoon, my treat?'

Plum stared at her. 'The Mandarin Oriental! Are you serious?'

Nellie grinned at her. 'I took the liberty of getting their brochure. She pushed it across the table to Plum. 'See which of their treatments you fancy! Then if we accidentally end up at a cocktail bar afterwards, telling rude stories, you can just blame it on me!' She suddenly turned to me. 'What do you say, Nat? Fancy bunking off school and coming with us?'

'Me? Seriously?' I was reeling. Plum and Nellie had never included me in their plans *ever*; they had definitely never suggested I bunked off school! I couldn't have been more astonished if Nellie had pulled out a packet of Rizlas and started smoking a joint! I tried to imagine being alone with my sisters in a grand upscale spa, being covered with seaweed or whatever they did to people at spas, and it was just too weird. At the same time I was genuinely touched.

'Thanks, but I don't think Jenny would let me go to

a cocktail bar,' I joked. 'Anyway, I don't want to miss the gym, seeing as Gus shelled out so much money for me to see a personal trainer.'

'You've really been bitten by the gym bug, haven't you?' Nellie said.

'I hated it at first,' I admitted. 'But Jacek's such a brilliant trainer he gets you to do all these things you think you can't do.'

'Natalie's got a cru-ush!' Plum sang, pointing at me.

'No I haven't!' I said indignantly. 'Jacek's ancient! He must be like thirty if he's a day!'

'Jacek isn't ancient!' Nellie said at once. 'I suppose you think Plum and I are ancient too!'

'Because you *are* ancient!' I teased.

'So who *have* you got a crush on?' Nellie asked.

'Why should you think I've got a crush on anyone?'

Plum gave me a sly grin. 'Nellie and I both noticed you're doing a lot of "dog walking" suddenly. We decided a boy was probably involved, didn't we, Nellie?'

'Almost certainly,' Nellie agreed, straight-faced.

'Well, there isn't.' But I could feel myself blushing so that both my sisters pointed accusing fingers at me.

'Ooh, you little fibber!' Plum said, laughing.

This conversation was so surprising it was making me slightly light-headed. I was right on the verge of telling my sisters all about my budding romance with Tom Nash, when Nellie's mobile went and she zoomed off into another room to take the call.

'Before I forget,' Plum said when she'd gone. 'I thought it would be more fun for you if you could bring a few friends along to the wedding. Maybe your Breakfast Club friends and anybody else who might be, you know, *special*!' She wiggled her eyebrows at me.

I gasped. 'I can really invite my friends! Plum, *thank* you! Oh, wow!' This was almost more surprising than my sisters inviting me along to a spa.

'If you give me their names now, I'll write out proper invitations,' Plum said, beaming. I had already seen the creamy invitation cards embossed with the names of Plum and her fiancé.

I gave her the names of everyone in the Breakfast Club, then because my sister seemed so convinced that I had a secret love life, I cheekily gave her Tom Nash's name before I went to fetch the dogs' leads.

'Tom Nash. So, that's what he's called?' Plum teased.

I'd finally got all the dogs on their leads straining to get out of the door, when on sudden impulse I called, 'Plum, would you mind adding Oliver Maybury to your guest list?'

'You do realise that makes five guests you're inviting?'

Plum said, sounding more like the old disapproving Plum. 'Who *is* Oliver Maybury anyway? Not another boyfriend?'

'You know Fiona Maybury who does those documentaries?' I called back. 'It's her son. And no, Oliver is not my boyfriend!'

'I didn't know you were friends with Fiona Maybury's son.' Plum sounded so impressed that I knew that Oliver was going to get his invitation.

Since I'd made up my mind not to talk to him ever again (not a hard resolution to keep seeing as he seemed to be going out of his way to avoid me), I had absolutely no idea why I'd just done that. I decided it must be Plum's wedding. It was making all of us act completely out of character, except my stepmother. She was as hostile and sour as always.

In the park I mentally replayed the conversation with my sisters. I wasn't sure which parts I was more amazed by; the fact that Plum and Nellie had talked to me like a normal human being, the fact that they had invited me along to their hen event at the Mandarin Oriental, or the fact that we had joked together about boys, almost like we were a normal family?

But now that I was out of the house I was remembering things I hadn't properly noticed at the time, like the way Nellie avoided answering when Plum asked her if she felt the same about Rupert as my elder sister felt about Gus. And there was something else; when Nellie's mobile went she gave a really guilty start before rushing away to take the call out of earshot. Normally when Nellie took calls she just talked loudly over everyone else regardless of who was listening, even when she was having a flirty conversation with Rupert.

This made me wonder about the identity of Nellie's mystery caller. Because if it was just a perfectly innocent call, why wouldn't my sister want us to hear?

I posted Lexie's wedding invitation on my way to school next day. I had the others in my bag to give to my friends; well, my friends plus Tom, my 'almost boyfriend'. I still hadn't made up my mind if I was going to give Oliver his. Every time I tried to imagine myself actually going up to him and handing it over, I found that I couldn't imagine what either of us would say next. I wasn't even sure why I wanted him there in the first place.

It's a peacemaking gesture, Natalie, I told myself. *And if Oliver is too petty-minded to accept, then it's no skin off your nose*.

But as I walked through the school gates, Oliver got

nudged to the back of my mind, because I'd suddenly remembered what day this was. This afternoon the judges of the fashion design competition were going to be announcing the winners in front of the whole school.

It was a lucky coincidence that this was also the day I just happened to bring my friends' invitations. When I eventually picked out Ella and Billie from the sea of blue and grey school uniforms I could see that Ella was already white with nerves.

I hurried over, already fishing out their invitations. 'Tada!' I crowed, waving the little cream envelopes under their noses. 'You'd SO better not be busy that day,' I added anxiously, 'because I'm relying on you guys to pick me up when I trip over Plum's train!'

'*No*!' Ella said, staring at her envelope with a stunned expression. 'No way!'

Billie practically snatched hers out of my hand. 'Is this what I think it is?'

I nodded. 'Plum asked if I'd like to invite some people.' I hadn't been sure if my friends would be pleased after all our recent hiccups, but they both started hugging me and going, 'Oh my GOD!'

'So you'll really come?' I asked tentatively.

'Are you *kidding*! Ella gasped. 'The Pegasus Hotel! You *bet* we're coming!'

'And obviously we want to support Nat, don't we, Ella!' Billie said, dead pan. 'I mean the Pegasus Hotel, that's just the icing on the cake, right?' Then she jumped up and down shrieking, '*The Pegasus Hotel*!! I can't believe we're getting to go there!'

'Woo-hoo! Plum is letting us come to her super-celeb wedding!' Ella squealed. People were turning to look by this time but she didn't care, she just waved her invitation in the air. 'Woo-hoo!' she shouted again. All the colour had come back to her cheeks.

'You're sure you didn't have to use threats or blackmail?' Billie asked me, laughing.

I shook my head. 'Nope! We'd all been sitting chatting in the kitchen and she just offered out of the blue.'

Billie almost choked. 'Hold up! Run that last bit by us again!'

'She just offered out of the blue?'

She shook her head. 'Uh-uh, just before. That bit about "sitting chatting in the kitchen"? Has Plum had a knock on the head recently, fallen off a piece of gym equipment or something?'

I laughed. 'Not that she's said!'

Ella and Billie were both staring at me in wonder.

'You were *seriously* all sitting round chatting. Like,

together?' Ella said just to make sure. 'Around the table. With Jenny?'

'No, God no! Just me, Plum and Nellie. Nellie actually invited me to bunk off school to go to the Mandarin Oriental with them for Plum's hen afternoon.'

My friends' jaws dropped.

'You're sure they were your real sisters?' Ella asked in awe. 'They hadn't been taken over by aliens?'

'Sounds more like Plum and Nellie have been taken over by humans!' Billie joked.

'What *is* going on!' Ella marvelled.

'I have no idea,' I told them truthfully. 'But Billie's about got it right. Both my sisters have started acting much more human. Well, Nellie went through a weird patch just after Plum and Gus announced their wedding, but now she seems almost, you know, *happy*.'

It had never occurred to me until that moment that Nellie had been unhappy, or that this might have something to do with why she was so often spiteful and mean.

'She's acting really weird though,' I confessed. 'Always zooming off somewhere in her MG Sports car, to meet friends she never ever mentioned before this, plus she constantly seems to be going to the gym.'

'*You* constantly go to the gym,' Ella pointed out.

We had started to drift towards the school building along with everybody else.

Billie gave me a wicked smile. 'You don't think she and Jacek . . . ?'

I gasped. 'Oh my God! That could be it!' Small clues suddenly started to slot together. 'When Plum asked Nellie if she was desperate to marry Rupert it was like she really didn't want to talk about him. That's when she invited me and Plum to go to the Mandarin Oriental. God, you don't think she's having a nervous breakdown?'

'I think she's doing some out-of-hours training with sexy Jacek and he's making her *really* happy!' Billie said, laughing.

'And she had that phone call,' I said almost to myself. I turned to the others. 'Her mobile went and she went scuttling into another room to take the call.'

I realised Ella had stopped listening. She'd gone pale again.

'What's wrong?' I asked her. 'You do know you're going to ace this competition, don't you?

'Oh my God!' she gasped, still gripped by some mystery horror. 'Billie, what are we going to *wear*!'

Billie looked blank. 'Wear to what?'

'To Plum's *wedding* of course!'

Billie shrugged. 'I only just got the invitation. I have no idea what I'm going to wear?'

'Then start thinking,' Ella ordered. 'This is going to be like the wedding of the year and I don't want us letting Natalie down.'

'We *won't*!' Billie said. 'Will we, Nat?'

'Of course you won't,' I said, hugging them.

But Ella, being Ella, wouldn't let it rest. Before we'd even reached our form room she had their outfits all worked out. Ella was going to wear a little short-sleeved 1960s style shift that she'd bought months ago but still hadn't had a chance to wear. I was with her when she bought it. It's a gorgeously subtle milky coffee colour with a fine oatmeal stripe, elegant but with just a tiny hint of boho. She was going to wear it with a statement bracelet and ivory-coloured ballet slippers. Billie was going to wear her loose cotton trousers with a silky top in glowing apricot and Ella was lending Billie her silver Egyptian style choker with the dark green stones.

'Phone Lexie at lunchtime so you can tell her that her invitation is in the post,' Ella said to me. 'Then she can talk us through what's in her wardrobe, so we can make sure our outfits harmonise with each other,' Ella said briskly as she dropped her bag down beside her desk.

'Ella!' Billie protested. 'You'll be making us wear co-ordinated undies next!'

'If necessary!' Ella flashed back. 'And that's a great idea!'

Billie grinned. 'Me and my big mouth.'

Our classmates were gradually settling in around us, jostling, teasing, swapping gossip. Then a ripple of laughter went through the room. Joe Grupetta had come in with his usual entourage of Marie Louise and the Alphas. Like everyone else, Joe was in school uniform. The top buttons of his shirt were left rakishly undone, and he had tied his tie so loosely that it looked more like a fashion accessory. He was also wearing his shades. When he saw us all looking he did a mocking bow. 'Good morning, losers! I'll send you a postcard from Paris.'

'Shouldn't you wait until the judges announce their decision? I don't think there are any losers yet!' Ella said, somehow keeping her cool.

'That's not the rumour I heard.' Joe gave her his trademark smirk following it up with an annoyingly fake laughing fit, making his shoulders shake. Ella just turned her back. I was glad I'd distracted her with the invitations. Caught up with thoughts about the wedding, she had been slightly more immune to Joe's taunts.

At lunchtime we phoned Lexie on my mobile (Billie and Ella had both run out of credit) and told her she was invited to Plum's wedding and her invitation was in the post. She took it so calmly I thought she'd misunderstood. 'Hang on,' she said, 'I just have to tell Bella.' Bella was the friend she got on with best at her school. For a minute we heard a buzz of voices and someone, presumably Bella, saying, 'The Pegasus Hotel! Oh my GOD, Lexie, you lucky thing! Well, you'd better at *least* bring me back some wedding cake!' Then we heard Bella and Lexie going, 'SQUEEEEEEE!'

We chatted to Lexie for a few minutes, pressing our ears to the phone trying to hear her over the usual playground din. Then I handed over to Ella so she could quiz Lexie about her wardrobe.

'Lexie says she'll ask her parents if they can take us in their people carrier,' Ella told Billie when she'd ended the call.

'So what have you told Lexie to wear?' Billie asked, amused.

'I didn't tell her what to wear, Billie! You make me sound like some kind of fashion tyrant!'

Billie looked innocently up at the sky. 'As if!'

Ella swatted her. 'I just told her what colours you and I were wearing and she decided, *totally* independently, Billie, actually, that she's going to wear that embroidered cream Indian style tunic she's got over cropped leggings. I suggested she could get some really pretty sparkly flip-flops from Accessorize and some bangles to complete her look.'

I found I could totally picture Lexie in the outfit Ella had described. 'You are so good at clothes,' I told her.

I hope I find out what I'm good at some day, I thought wistfully. But I didn't say this out loud because Ella really didn't need me bringing her down with my own insecurity today of all days.

Today afternoon lessons ended promptly at 2.45 and all the classes gradually filed into the hall with their teachers.

I heard someone behind me grumble, 'I suppose this is yet another one of Mrs Spelling's attempts to turn education into light entertainment!' I looked round and saw Mrs Gildersleeve or as we call her, the Fun Police, looking daggers at the judges who were making their way up on stage.

'She's miffed because she wasn't asked to be a judge,' Ella hissed.

The judges, Josh Berolli, Miss Tempest our history teacher and Mrs Spelling, took their places under a brightly coloured banner with the name of our school and the words Fashion Competition in huge glittering letters. Mrs Spelling laid out five portfolios on the table in front of the judges. The portfolios were just coloured card. That way nobody could tell by just looking at them whose work was whose.

Joe and his supporters had all bagged seats in the middle of the front row. I wondered how anyone got to be that confident. It was like he'd made up his mind he'd won, and now all he had to do was sit back and wait. Maybe some people were just born winners, I thought. But how could you bear to be a winner if you'd cheated?

Ella kept swallowing as if she felt sick.

'Not long now, honey,' Billie told her.

'Yeah, Ella, you've done all you can,' I said, squeezing her hand, which felt clammy with nerves.

Having conferred one last time with the other judges, Mrs Spelling stood up and smiled at everyone. 'I would like to welcome you to our first ever fashion design competition. I say first because I'm sure it won't be the last. My fellow judges and I have been thrilled and astonished at the sophistication and originality of the designs we have seen in these entries.'

Joe turned round to mouth, 'Loser,' at Ella.

'I want to thank everyone for submitting such wonderful work and raising the bar for the standard of design work in this school. It would be wonderful if you could all be winners, and in future years it wouldn't surprise me if some of you who had to be eliminated this time turn out to be future winners. From next week all the entries to the competition will be on display in the foyer so even if you don't win this time, everyone will get to see your work.'

'Oh, please just get *on* with it, woman!' Billie muttered.

This was so unlike my old school, I can't tell you. No 'bright but not brilliant' comments here. You could see that soft-hearted Mrs Spelling was absolutely dreading having to disappoint the kids who didn't make the final cut.

She went on to name the runners-up, who were Fareeda, Marie Louise, and Alice Hobbs. Everybody clapped and the three girls ran up to get their gift tokens from Josh Berolli.

Mrs Spelling waited until the applause had died

down and all the runners-up were back in their seats. 'Right now we've reached the really manicure-ruining part!' she joked. She turned to Josh Berolli and he picked out one of the portfolios, carefully sliding out some of the sketches.

'I should explain that we've been faced with a real dilemma,' Mrs Spelling said. 'Our task was to come up with one overall winner, but all the judges agreed that two of the entrants really stood out head and shoulders above the others, for freshness, originality – and, most importantly when you are designing a school uniform, practicality. So we decided that we had no choice but to have two winners! Mr Berolli, can we please have the first winner?'

Josh Berolli smilingly held up the first set of sketches, realised he was holding them the wrong side out and quickly turned them around. 'And the first of our two overall winners is—' he said, leaving a teasing pause like the judges on the X Factor. 'Joe Grupetta!'

Joe jumped out of his seat and made his way up to the stage.

Mrs Spelling started going on about how Joe's designs were fun and young but also timeless and totally wearable, but I had stopped listening. I have unusually good eyesight (It's a Bonneville-St John thing) and I'd noticed something that nobody else had noticed, not even Ella. I'd spotted them the moment Josh Berolli held up the sketches that were supposedly Joe's. The backs of the sketches were covered with doodles of tiny interlinked hearts.

I jumped up from my seat, urgently waving my hand. 'Stop, please stop! Joe didn't do those designs. Ella Swanson did!'

Joe froze in the middle of reaching out to shake Josh Berolli's hand then spun around with a face like thunder. 'Of course I did them. Are you sick?'

'No and I'm not a cheat either,' I flashed back. 'You stole those designs from Ella and I can prove it'

The whole school had turned to look at me. Even normally this would give me wobbly knees, and I felt myself shaking like a leaf.

'You're bluffing,' Joe sneered. 'You can't prove anything because there's nothing to prove.'

'It's true, let me show you,' I appealed to the judges, willing my legs to hold up for long enough to see justice done.

All the judges looked impatient and uncomfortable but they nodded.

I tottered up on to the stage and turned over the sketches so that the judges could see Ella's repeated doodles on the back.

'You see these linked hearts?' I told them shakily. 'Ella puts them on everything. She doesn't even know she's drawing them. When she's a proper fashion designer it's going to be her logo. If you look you'll see them on the back of all her drawings. And does that look like the kind of doodle a boy would do?' I asked the judges. 'Does it?'

Scandalised whispers started to spread through the hall. Then a scornful voice rang out, summing up what everybody was thinking. 'You are SO busted, Joe Grupetta!' Billie told him with intense satisfaction.

I shakily made my way back to my friends, collapsing gratefully into my seat. Then of course I had to stand up again to let Ella go up to receive her prize.

'Well, Ella,' said Mrs Spelling, still trying to pulling herself together. 'I'm not sure if you noticed, but we never got around to actually announcing the second winner! This is all quite extraordinary but now that Mr Grupetta is out of the running, it seems that you, my dear, have actually won twice over!'

'Oh, my God,' Billie whispered.

Ella didn't say a word. I don't think she could really take it in.

'Congratulations, Ella!' Mrs Spelling said, laughing.

'You've won yourself a trip to Paris! And one of your designs will be replacing the girls' regular winter uniform.'

Ella still looked dazed as she shook all the judges' hands, then she walked back to her seat through a storm of applause, and hugged me in front of everybody. 'Thank you,' she said, fighting her tears. 'Thank you so much, Natalie.'

'Who knew our Nat could be that fierce!' Billie teased as we slowly made our way out of the hall. 'Maybe she should go to law school?' she said to Ella. 'I can really see her in a wig, can't you?

Ella grinned. '"Does that look like the kind of doodle a boy would do, milud!" You were pretty amazing, Nat!'

'I don't like cheats and bullies,' I said. 'And Joe Grupetta is a cheat *and* a bully. You worked so hard, Ella. I couldn't stand by and let him just take the credit. Plus it was really all down to spotting your logo.' As soon as I saw that I had to speak up for Ella. I didn't have a choice.

I suddenly spotted Oliver up ahead. 'Don't go away,' I said abruptly. I raced off to catch him before he zoomed off to study with whichever private tutor he was seeing tonight. 'Hi,' I said breathlessly.

'Oh, yes, hi,' Oliver said awkwardly.

'I just wanted to give you this!' I held out one of Plum's plush, creamy envelopes. 'Plum said I could invite some friends to her wedding, so obviously I wanted to invite you.'

'Thanks,' Oliver said coldly. 'But I think I might be busy that day.'

'You don't know what day it is yet?' I pointed out, giggling.

'I just, I think I might be busy for quite a while,' he said, carefully avoiding my eyes.

I knew I'd hurt Oliver's feelings but I still thought I could put things right with a Nat-type joke. 'Busy doing what?' I teased. 'Or has protecting Eva from her evil boyfriend turned into like, your full-time job! Come *on*,' I wheedled. 'I thought we were friends?'

'Yes, so did I,' said Oliver, and he just walked away, leaving me stupidly clutching my invitation.

'I hope you've got one of those for me!' Tom Nash had come up behind me. As usual his cool blue stare didn't give much away. I could feel my face still burning from what had just happened and wondered how much Tom had heard. With a massive effort I shifted into flirt mode. 'Strangely enough I think I *might* just have a spare invitation somewhere,' I said, pretending to think.

He shook his head, tossing his beautiful black hair over his eyes. 'Forget "spare invitation"!' he said scornfully. 'If Oliver Maybury gets a personal invite, I want a personal invite.'

'Just as well I've got one then, isn't it?' Still numb at how Oliver had treated me, I watched in a daze as Tom tore open the envelope on the spot and immediately started scanning the card inside. '*Whoa!* So it really is at the Pegasus!' he exclaimed.

'How did you know about that?' I asked, startled.

'Are you kidding? Just about everybody probably heard! Your friends didn't exactly bother keeping their voices down,' he said carelessly. 'Anyway, you can tell "Plum," he added with a smirk, 'that I definitely accept!'

'I'll tell her.' It occurred to me that Tom might not have accepted so enthusiastically if my sister's wedding was being held somewhere less upscale. Though my friends were over the moon at the chance to go inside the famous Pegasus, I knew they'd have come even if we'd been holding it in a real dive.

Just then Ella came up to me still glowing from her big success. 'Sorry to interrupt, Nat, but I'm meeting my mum in a few minutes and I wanted to ask you something before I go.'

'Sure, ask away,' I said.

'I wondered if you might be able to make it to Mario's for Billie's Friday night gig? I know it's the night before the wedding but if Plum doesn't need you, I thought we could meet up. Lexie's coming and it would be so much more fun if you came too.'

'I'll definitely come!' The words jumped out of my mouth as if they'd just been waiting. 'We can celebrate you getting your first foot on the ladder of fashion fame!'

Ella's eyes lit up. 'Honestly? Oh, that's brilliant, Nat! Billie will be so pleased!'

'What kind of session is Billie's doing?' Tom asked in obvious surprise.

'She's got the early DJ slot at Mario's,' I told him.

'I didn't know she was a budding DJ.' He sounded miffed, like he'd been deliberately kept out of the loop.

'She isn't a *budding* anything,' Ella said fiercely. 'She's an actual DJ and she's brilliant.'

'I might bring a few friends along myself,' Tom said just as if Ella hadn't spoken. 'I'm off home now,' he added, turning to give me his special knee-melting stare. 'Are you coming? Seeing as we're going in the same direction?'

I didn't always *like* Tom Nash that much but I did

find him really hard to resist. 'OK,' I told him, avoiding Ella's eyes. 'I just need to drop something off. I'll be two minutes tops.'

I'd been planning to rip up Oliver's invitation into a million tiny pieces and drop it in the nearest bin. But then I thought I'd give him just one more chance and secretly slip it into his locker (Oliver was constantly forgetting to bring his locker key so ended up mostly leaving it unlocked). I thought maybe when he saw that I'd taken the trouble to actually deliver his invitation he might have a last minute change of heart?

When I tried the door of his locker it immediately swung open. I half chucked the wedding invitation inside then bent to shut the door. I was surprised to see a tiny photo stuck on the back. Oliver had never struck me as the kind of person to decorate the inside of his locker. Seized by an unexpected jolt of jealousy, I crouched down to get a good look at this irritating girl who meant so much to Oliver that he wanted to see her face every single time he looked in his locker.

My eyes slowly widened as I realised the girl was me.

Chapter Ten

Next morning all through our maths lesson with Mr Malik I kept thinking, *Has he found it yet?* Then it was, *He must have found it by now.*

If he had he didn't say anything. He wasn't out-and-out blanking me. Oliver never played those kinds of games. If our paths crossed, he just nodded and said quietly, 'Hello, Natalie,' then kept on walking.

It wasn't true what Billie said, that I didn't like Oliver because he was so nice. It was more like I couldn't see why somebody like him would care about somebody like me. Oliver was so totally himself while I was still floundering around like a fish out of water figuring out who I was supposed to be.

When I got back from my last but one gym session, I was surprised to find my sisters in the kitchen all glowing and sweet-smelling from their afternoon at the

Mandarin Oriental. There was a tall bottle of fizzy water on the table between them and two glasses.

'Hi, you,' said Plum so warmly that I had to stop myself turning round to see if someone had walked in behind me.

'Hi,' I said cautiously. 'I thought you guys were going on to have cocktails and tell rude drunken jokes and kiss policemen?'

'Nah,' said Nellie, laughing, 'I was up for it – especially the policeman part,' she added with a grin, 'but Plum was determined to be a boring old married lady.' She sounded surprisingly cheerful about it I thought.

'So did you have a good time being hens?' I asked them.

'Fabulous. We must take you with us next time. Actually, we brought you back a pressie.' Plum pushed a pretty carrier bag towards me. Inside were some little packages of spa products wrapped in tissue and a tiny scented candle that smelled like heaven.

'Oh, *thank* you,' I breathed. 'You didn't have to do that!'

'We thought you might like to have your own mini spa experience at home,' Nellie said.

'I'll do it tomorrow night,' I said, still blissfully

sniffing my candle. 'Before I go to see Billie do her DJ set at Mario's.'

'Is *he* going to be there?' Plum asked at once. 'You know, that boy you see when you go out "dog walking"?'

'*No!*' I said. 'I keep telling you there *is* no "he". Where's Jenny by the way?' I asked quickly to get off the subject of boys.

'Probably out playing bridge,' Plum said carelessly. 'Nellie and I thought we'd go out for an Indian later.' She poured herself another glass of fizzy water. 'Do you fancy coming?'

This was turning out to be another one of those astonishing conversations. The idea of Plum and Nellie actually eating for pleasure was like Jacek and smiling. You just couldn't imagine them being in the same sentence like I couldn't imagine myself sitting with my sisters nibbling poppadums to a never-ending Bollywood track. So I fibbed and told them I'd already had a snack on the way back from the gym.

'Come and keep us company then,' Nellie suggested. 'Oh, do come, Nat! Plum and I won't be around to bug you for ever, you know!'

Part of me genuinely wanted to go sailing off to the restaurant with them, the three Bonneville-St John sisters. We'd be like the family I'd always wanted.

Maybe I'd wanted it too long, because now my wish was finally coming true, I simply didn't trust it. I couldn't shake the feeling that any minute my stepmother would burst in with some scornful remark and ruin everything as always.

'Maybe we could do it another time?' I suggested.

'Sure,' said Plum. 'Preferably before Gus and I go off to Singapore though, hey, little sister?'

Nellie had got a text. She did that annoying smirk people do when they read texts, and quickly sent one back.

'Was that your faithful Rupert?' Plum asked her.

'Hmm?' Nellie looked as if she'd been miles away. 'No, somebody else,' she said vaguely.

'So, Nellie, when do you actually go to train with Jacek, because I never see you at the gym?' I said cheekily. This was true. I had bumped into my older sister a few times but never Nellie. I watched closely to see if she blushed.

'You wouldn't have seen me because I go really early on the way to work,' Nellie said calmly. 'It's nice and empty then.' And though I was carefully scrutinising her for signs of guilt I didn't detect even a tiny flush of pink. *Billie must have got it wrong*, I thought and I was slightly disappointed. I had quite enjoyed the idea of my sister having a scandalous fling with the mysterious unsmiling Jacek.

'You're sure we can't persuade you?' Nellie picked up her bag.

I shook my head. 'Not this time. I've got some homework to finish then I want to try out that fabulous face-pack you got me so I'll look my best for Mario's tomorrow.'

'Is that boy you invited to the wedding, Tom Nash, going to be at Mario's?' Plum asked, totally having a stab in the dark, and suddenly I was blushing enough for all three of us!

'No. Well, he might go, but he's going with a group of friends. We're not actually going there *together or anything.*'

Nellie wagged her finger at me. 'Our little sister's growing up, Plum.'

'It doesn't seem two minutes since she was dragging her disgusting pink blanky around.' Plum gave a nostalgic sigh.

'Oh, yeah, thanks for reminding me. I must remember to leave that behind when I go to Mario's,' I said tartly.

Both my sisters laughed with surprise. They were still laughing as they hurried off to the restaurant. It was like, with that one remark, I'd lost my little sister status and become one of them.

Next day, Oliver didn't come to school. I should explain that Oliver is never ill. The only other time I'd known him to take a day off school was when he had to go to some award ceremony with Fiona because one of her documentaries was up for a prize.

'He probably had a dentist's appointment,' Ella suggested. 'He might still show up for afternoon school.'

By this time I had told my friends about being such a total cow to him (embarrassingly they'd kind of already figured that out), also about finding my picture in his locker, which made Ella and Billie both clutch at their hearts and go, 'Oh my God, that is so *sweet*!'

At lunchtime I thought I'd caught a glimpse of his curly hair coming in through the door of the dinner hall, then my stomach clenched as I saw that it was actually someone else.

'Hey, cheer up, Natty!' Ella said, giving me a little shake. 'In just a few hours we're all going to be partying at the Pegasus!'

'Yay,' I said.

'Let's try that again but with more feeling, shall we?' Billie said sternly.

'YAY!' I tried then I let out a groan. 'Oh, God, you guys. I'm so glad you're going to be there for backup. I don't think I could face it if you weren't coming.'

'Luckily you don't have to worry, because we are coming and you're going to be the most perfect bridesmaid in the history of bridesmaids, isn't she, Billie?' Ella said loyally.

I tried to remember why I had been so obsessed with being a perfect bridesmaid, when now the only thing on my mind was finding out what had happened to Oliver.

Lunchtime came and went and he still didn't show up.

'You don't think it's because of me?' I asked my friends anxiously as we mooched around at afternoon break.

'Because everything that goes wrong is your fault, right?' Billie patted my hand to take the sting out of the tease. 'Famine, Plagues of frogs, the recession, it's all down to Natalie Bonneville-St John!'

'*You* think there's something wrong too, don't you!' I said.

'He's probably just got a cold, or his mum's won a BAFTA or something,' Ella comforted me.

I shook my head. 'They do the BAFTAS at night.'

'A cold then.'

'He never gets colds,' I told them.

'Final proof that Oliver Maybury is superhuman,' Billie joked, then saw my expression and said quickly, 'though a very sweet and lovely superhuman obviously!'

For the millionth time I checked my mobile to see if Oliver might have left me a message, which was a dumb thing to do, even for me, seeing that Oliver had hardly texted me even when we were speaking, plus his phone was almost always out of credit.

Something's happened, I thought. I couldn't explain to my friends that this wasn't just me thinking the worst. I just knew in the churning pit of my stomach that something *really* bad had happened to Oliver.

Mario's at night had a totally different atmosphere to the daylight Mario's. Some of this was down to the crowd, which was noticeably younger and livelier than the Saturday morning breakfast crowd (not counting the extremely young and lively Breakfast Clubbers obviously!). Some of it was down to all the little candle lamps glimmering all along the bar and on the tables, but most of it was down to Billie and her music.

It was strange at first to see my friend standing over her decks with her heavy duty headphones on. In contrast to the music, she seemed still and quiet as she concentrated on keeping her set flowing, mixing tunes so skilfully that they were like one seamless piece of music, sometimes dancing, rapt, her eyes closed, as if the music was actually being channelled through her. Once she lifted her arms at the crucial moment in the tune and I actually felt the energy in the café go zooming right up through the roof.

I'd seen Billie performing her own music at the benefit, but this was the first time I'd see her DJ. *She's like a different person*, I thought. Standing behind her decks with all these people watching, she seemed untouchable, like a stranger, totally beyond my reach. Then she suddenly looked in our direction, saw us all waving and flashed a huge grin.

At that moment I felt the music lift me out of my depression, and some tight knot of worry magically dissolved. Like my friends, I suddenly found myself up on my feet though I couldn't remember actually deciding to dance! Nothing else mattered as Ella, Lexie and I danced and danced inside our golden bubble of candle-light. Though Billie was physically sealed off from us behind her decks with her headphones on, she didn't seem separate to us now. It felt like we were all part of the same dance.

At one point I half noticed Tom Nash coming in with his friends. I saw him look meaningfully in my direction. I had a feeling he expected me to go over, but I didn't fancy walking up to him in front of all his friends. Instead I gave him a wave and went back to our table, where I thirstily finished off my soft drink. The dancing had made me parched.

Billie had reached the quietest part of her set now before she started revving up again for her big finale, so we took the chance to catch up with Lexie. Ella commented that she looked happier than she'd seemed for a while.

She grinned. 'Have I been *that* much of a grouse! Don't answer that, Natalie!' she joked.

'Hey, I had it coming,' I told her.

'I'm so glad you could come to see Billie, especially as it's the night before the big wedding,' Lexie said.

'I'm glad I came to see her too,' I said, grinning.

'Isn't she amazing?' Ella said. 'You totally can't describe it, can you? You have to like, *see* her in action!

I nodded. 'She's incredible.'

Ella went off to get everybody fresh Cokes and I said, 'So how are things at home, Lexie?'

'Really good,' she said, beaming. 'It really was just a phase, like you said. Kathy and Will had a long talk and they decided they need to change their work–life balance. Kathy said ever since the recession all they ever do is work or do child care or chores and all the like, *fun* things they used to do together before they started up Sweet World, had got totally squeezed out.'

'So what are they going to do?'

'Will's already done it!' she said with a broad grin. 'He's booked them both a weekend at some fancy hotel in Bath and they're going to just laze around and eat good food and wander around all those cool little shops. You know Bath is where they first met?'

'So it's kind of like a second honeymoon?'

'It totally is! Oh, Nat, it's *such* a relief, I can't tell you! I was imagining all these terrible things but absolutely none of them happened, phew!' Lexie wiped imaginary sweat off her brow, laughing at herself.

'Who's going to look after your little brothers though?' I asked, knowing that Lexie quite often ended up picking up the slack.

'My gran,' she said promptly. 'She's completely over her hip operation now and she says she's really happy to help out.'

'Who's really happy to help out?' Ella had come back with our drinks.

'Lexie's grandmother!' I told her. 'Lexie's mum and

dad are going off to Bath for a second honeymoon.' I felt as chuffed as if I'd arranged it myself. I had helped Lexie through a bad patch (she had virtually told me so), and now everything in their family was happily back to normal.

I pushed back my chair. 'I'm just off to the little girls' room.'

'Good luck with that!' Ella said. 'There was a massive queue last time I looked.'

We were having to shout at each other now. Billie had reached the wildest part of her set. I could feel the bass-line coming up through my feet and jolting up my spine as I went off to join the queue which was snaking back almost halfway around the café.

Lexie suddenly came running up and squeezed in behind me. 'I didn't want to go until you said!' she shouted. 'My bladder came out in sympathy!' After a couple of minutes she said, 'Blow this, we'll be queuing all night. I'm using the gents! Coming?'

I had never in my entire life gone into the gents but Lexie had a quick peek before she let me follow her in, then we quickly beetled into our stalls and bolted the doors.

Almost the minute I had locked my door, I heard people coming in; I mean people as in guys! I was so appalled I couldn't actually do what I'd come into the gents to do. Then I thought; *What are you panicking about, Natalie? Just keep quiet until they go away.*

The guys (it sounded like there were three or four) had come in all joshing and competing with each other like boys do, then I totally froze behind my door as I suddenly heard Tom's voice. 'Hey, that's enough! I won't hear a word against her! I know Natalie used to look like a disco granny, but now she's lost all that weight you've got to admit she doesn't look *that* bad. Anyway, I've got to be nice to her now, haven't I?'

'Oh, yeah, because you've been invited to the Pegasus Hotel!' someone jeered.

'Sweet!' said someone else.

'Anyway, it's not like I have to make any effort,' Tom added. 'Natalie's basically a one-girl chat show! I just have to like, nod every now and then and smile like this!' I think he must have demonstrated his sexy smile because all his friends started braying with laughter.

I was huddling on the loo, going hot and cold and wondering if it was possible for a person to actually die of pure shame, when I heard a metal bolt shoot back as Lexie burst out of her stall like a ninja. There were suppressed gasps and frantic zipping sounds from the boys.

I heard my friend say coldly, 'Hey, you! Yes you with the hair! I wouldn't bother turning up to the Pegasus if I were you, not unless you actually want to be kicked into the Thames? For your information, scum-bag, Natalie is one of the most beautiful girls I know. The real question is what she ever saw in a total slime-ball like you!' I heard the main door slam as Lexie stormed out into the café.

I waited until the boys left, mumbling sheepishly about how girls shouldn't be allowed to lurk in the boys' toilets, then I made my way back to my friends in a state of utter confusion. On the one hand I was feeling totally humiliated. On the other hand, I thought, I couldn't have asked for a better revenge!

By the time I reached our table Lexie had already explained the situation to Ella and they both greeted me with sympathetic looks.

'No, really, I'm fine,' I told them. 'OK, so I could have probably done without the "disco granny" bit,' I admitted.

'You *never* looked like a disco granny,' Ella said fiercely. 'Tom Nash is a knob!'

'Ella!' I said.

'Well, he *is*!' she said and suddenly we were laughing so hard we were practically weeping. What made it even more hilarious was seeing Tom warily looking our way, obviously freaked by the hoots of laughter coming from our table. He knew we were laughing at him and I don't think Tom was used to being laughed at, not by girls anyway.

When I could finally speak, I told Ella, 'Lexie was SO awesome. I wish I'd seen her exploding out of the toilet like the vengeful angel!'

'So do I!' Ella said, still crying with laughter.

'I'm surprised Tom didn't have a heart attack on the spot!' I said in that high-pitched voice you get when you're trying not to laugh and we all went off into a new fit of hysterics. Then we remembered that we were here to support Billie and pulled ourselves together.

'I actually thought you'd be a lot more upset.' Lexie had to put her head close to me and Ella's so we could hear what she was saying.

'You'd think so, wouldn't you,' I shouted.

OK, so my pride had been a bit dented. It would be a while before I'd get over that 'disco granny' insult. But it was dawning on me that my romance with Tom, if that's what it was, had never been real. Like actors in a movie, we were always playing a part. Tom was the Judd Nelson character, the sexy boy with the dodgy past, and I was the mixed-up posh girl who was only just learning how to flirt.

But Oliver and me, that was real.

That was my last coherent thought before Billie's sounds lifted us up out of our seats and drove us out into the middle of the café to dance our cares away.

Chapter Eleven

On the day of my sister's wedding I woke at dawn, which I saw, looking at my alarm clock in dismay, was around 3.30 am. I put a pillow over my head to block out the birdsong echoing deafeningly around Kensington Square and might actually have succeeded in going back to sleep if the four police cars, three fire engines and at least two ambulances hadn't gone shrieking and wailing past on the high street like the Emergency Vehicles of the Apocalypse as my dad calls them. At five I gave up pretending and trudged downstairs to make myself a cup of tea.

When I walked into the kitchen, I jumped out of my skin to see Plum sitting at the kitchen table, like a ghost in her white nightdress. Her hands were wrapped around a steaming mug of hot water with a slice of lemon and her face was as white as her nightie. All the dogs had come to lie at her feet with worried expressions.

'Wedding nerves?' I asked sympathetically.

My sister gave me a tight nod. 'Feel really sick.'

She must have stayed the night in her old room, I realised, something about it being bad luck for the bride groom to see his bride on their wedding day before the actual ceremony.

'Would you rather just be by yourself?' I asked.

She shook her head so I made a pot of builder's tea for me and came to sit opposite her at the table.

'I was just lying in bed thinking I'll probably never sleep in my room again,' Plum said in a choked voice.

'You don't sleep there anyway,' I said tactlessly.

'That's so not the point,' she wailed. 'I know I can if I want to. Everything's changing, Nat, and I'm really scared!'

'Oh, *Plum*.' I got up and put my arms around her. She let me hug her for about five seconds then she started hunting for a tissue and said, 'I know I'm being silly.'

'Can I join the party!' Nellie came in wearing a T-shirt and sleep shorts. She peered dubiously into Plum's mug. 'Want a tea bag in that hot water, sweetie?'

'She's feeling sick,' I said. 'There's some real tea in the pot.'

Nellie nodded. 'I'm not surprised you're feeling sick. It's a big thing saying your "I dos" in front of the whole world. Not having second thoughts?'

Plum looked outraged. 'No, of *course* not!'

'I was just saying,' Nellie said. 'Because if you are – having second thoughts, I mean – it would be much better to tell him now rather than to leave it till the honeymoon.'

Plum just gave her a look and Nellie quickly held up her hands. 'OK, OK. It's just that . . .'

'Just what?' Plum snapped nervously.

Nellie pulled a face. 'I maybe should have told you before. I just didn't want to cast, you know, a dark shadow over your happiness, but Rupert and I broke up so he definitely won't be coming to your wedding.'

Plum's eyes went wide. 'Oh my God, Nellie! Are you OK?'

'I'm fine,' she said cheerfully. 'I wasn't quite so great at the time he dumped me though!'

'He *dumped* you!' Plum and I echoed in horror.

Nellie pulled a face. 'The night you and Gus got engaged. Not great timing. Anyway, sweetie, I just wanted to get that out of the way. But I am really and truly fine. I actually feel like I've had a lucky escape. This is going to sound mad but in some ways I think I only went out with Rupert because you were going out with Gus.'

I could see Plum was still fuming at the thought of Rupert dumping Nellie. 'I never really liked him, you know,' she said abruptly. 'Something about his eyes; he always looked so kind of – *smug*.'

Nellie's mouth dropped open. 'You never said!'

'Nobody says anything in this house,' I commented. 'Haven't you noticed?'

'Now that you mention it,' Nellie said drily. 'Nat, do you think you could make another pot? This tea's stewed, and I could *kill* for a slice of toast.'

'Oh, yes please!' Plum said unexpectedly. Nellie's news seemed to have shocked the queasiness out of her.

I made tea and several rounds of toast, setting out plates and butter and some home-made gooseberry jam that Jenny had bought at a Women's Institute sale in Norfolk last summer when we were in Norfolk.

Without too much effort we managed to demolish the entire plate of toast between us. Then Plum looked at her watch and raced to the door yelling, 'Oh *God*! The hairdresser will be here in half an hour and I haven't had a shower or washed my hair!' Then she flew back to me and Nellie and hugged us, for a good ten seconds this time, and said, 'It'll be OK, won't it? Tell me it'll be OK?'

Then we all flinched in surprise as the doorbell rang. The hairdresser had arrived half an hour early and our special sisterly moment was over.

Nellie and I rushed about like people in one of those jerky old-fashioned movies, having showers, washing and drying our hair, putting on our bridesmaids' dresses, letting people in (the woman who was going to do all our make-up, Gus's sister who was personally hand-delivering Plum's wedding bouquet and the flower crowns for the bridesmaids) and letting the hairdresser out, then sprinting up to the bathroom to get my make-up done.

I couldn't believe it when I looked in the mirror and saw what the make-up artist had done to my face. She had put so much gunk on my eyes I could barely move my eyelids. Then I saw Nellie and she looked just as bad! 'She's made us look like thirty-year-old *hookers*!' I hissed.

She laughed. 'It's got to show up from a long way off, remember.'

'They'll be able to see these eyes on Mars,' I said darkly, secretly enjoying making her laugh.

Then Nellie got another text from the mysterious

man who wasn't Rupert, and wandered off to read it in private.

Aunt Clare arrived with my Uncle Stephen and their five children. Matilda was already wearing her bridesmaid's dress and was walking with a very straight back and a calm queenly expression. When Nellie carefully placed the fragile crown of flowers on my little cousin's head everybody went, 'Aah,' even Jenny, because Matilda looked so cute.

My dad was handing out drinks to our guests, and being such a real sweetie that I couldn't help wishing he could be like that all the time, not only when one of his daughters was getting married or needing to be rescued from boarding school hell.

Then Nellie called us all into the hall in time to see Plum shyly descending the stairs looking like a royal bride in her simple Grace Kelly style wedding dress with the long floating train, and a veil of gauzy white lace.

That's when it sank in that this was real. My sister was really getting married and really going away to live in a foreign country thousands of miles away from Kensington Square.

There was no time to think about this though as the special wedding limo was outside waiting for Plum.

Nellie and I helped my sister into the back, carefully arranging her train so it wouldn't get crushed. Then she went off with my father, who looked very calm and dignified in his wedding suit. Jenny was travelling to the Pegasus Hotel with some of the Norfolk relatives. Nellie and I squeezed into the back-row of my aunt and uncle's old Renault Espace beside Matilda and a couple of my older cousins.

When I finally climbed out of the Espace, I was overjoyed to see Oliver waiting patiently outside the Pegasus.

'I didn't think you'd come,' I said, amazed, then a brisk wind snatched at my crown of flowers. Oliver made a lucky grab with his left hand, which was when I noticed that his right hand was totally encased in plaster.

'I knew how much the wedding meant to you,' he said gruffly, handing me my crown back. 'It would have been churlish not to come.'

I had to fight my smiles. Oliver Maybury is probably the only boy I know who uses words like 'churlish'. 'So what happened to your hand?' I asked.

He shrugged. 'Just one of those things. They always say ninety-nine per cent of accidents happen in the home.'

My eyes went wide. 'Ninety-nine per cent! Is it really that much?'

'I have no idea,' he said with a grin. 'I just made it up!'

'Natalie!' Nellie called.

'Uh-oh!' I said. 'I'll catch up with you later, Oliver!'

I scurried off to help Nellie get both Plum and her mile-long train out of the limo with as much dignity and as few creases as possible.

Then Daddy took Plum's arm and we set off into the hotel, with Nellie and I walking behind them carefully holding on to Plum's train and Matilda walking beside us clutching her posy, and giving us occasional little grins.

We walked through the vast foyer, past fascinated strangers who stopped to snap pictures with their mobiles. Two men wearing the Pegasus Hotel livery were already waiting by some double doors, which they flung open for us as if we really were royalty. On the other side of the doors was a sunlit space crowded with people, who all turned, smiling, in their seats, wanting a first glimpse of the bride.

In a kind of dream I heard the opening chords of the music Plum and Gus had chosen and suddenly we were all moving off, as perfectly in step as if we'd been doing this all our lives, slowly making our way past the familiar faces of relatives – also people I'd never seen in my life – and suddenly I saw Ella, Billie and Lexie in the same row of seats as Oliver all beaming encouraging smiles at me.

Having begun by dreading the whole thing, I found myself loving every dream-like step; the silky slithery rustle of Plum's train, the feeling of my own dress swishing against my ankles, and the fairytale feeling of wearing a crown of sweet-scented flowers – I suddenly wanted it to last for ever.

Slowly, deliberately, we moved closer and closer to Gus and his best man and the jolly grey-haired woman who was conducting their wedding ceremony. Gus suddenly turned to look at his bride and I saw his totally ordinary face light up. At that moment he seemed almost handsome in his morning suit with a silvery grey tie to match our silvery-grey dresses. He looked so thrilled to be getting married that for a minute I thought he was going to come sprinting to meet us to hurry things along. But he just waited, smiling and patient, for Plum to reach his side.

Then, just as she got close enough to touch, he leaned towards her, whispering something into her veil that only my sister could hear and though I couldn't see her face, I could tell she was laughing.

After all the build-up, the actual ceremony seemed to be over in a flash. Plum and Gus made their vows in clear steady voices and the jolly grey-haired lady told Gus he could now kiss the bride. 'Like he never did *that* before!' Nellie said in my ear. Gus gave my sister a long and passionate kiss and I heard my friends give a loud cheer and saw my stepmother shoot them a sour look.

My sister was safely married. I had been a bridesmaid and survived! But though the hard part was over, my bridesmaid's duties weren't, not yet.

Now we all had to go out onto the hotel lawn to be photographed by the willows. After that Nellie and I had the delicate operation of carefully folding and detaching Plum's train while she babbled to us that she was so happy and we had been the best bridesmaids any bride could ever have. Then Plum noticed that Nellie was cradling her train in her arms like a precious newborn baby and got the giggles. Then Nellie ran off to take the rolled-up fabric to the concierge for safe-keeping and finally I was free!

Picking up my skirts, I rushed to find my friends somewhere in the sea of chattering wedding guests. They took it in turn to hug me, then Ella quickly straightened my floral crown, which had come askew.

'You *did* it!' she said, beaming.

'You didn't look even a bit nervous!' Billie told me.

Lexie nodded. 'You were as calm as if your sister got married every day.'

'Plum looked SO terrified when you all first came in!' Ella told me.

'Did she, honestly?' I said in surprise.

Billie grinned. 'Like a baby rabbit in the headlights! Then Gus whispered whatever he whispered and you could see her almost start to enjoy herself.'

I was anxiously scanning faces as we talked. 'I can't see Oliver.'

'He was here a minute ago,' Lexie said.

'I heard him mutter something about not having breakfast and going to find the food,' Billie remembered.

'Can you believe that boy broke his hand inside his own house?' I said, giggling. 'Talk about accident prone!'

I saw my friends exchange looks. 'Did Oliver happen to mention *how* he broke his hand?' Ella asked carefully.

I shook my head. 'He just said it was one of those things.'

Lexie did a weird spluttering laugh. 'I wouldn't call

having some maniac charging into your house "just one of those things"!'

'What!'

My friends all nodded.

'Eva's boyfriend tried to force his way into their house to talk to Eva,' Ella said. 'So Oliver thumped him and knocked him out cold!'

'Way to go, Oliver!' Billie said, grinning.

I couldn't seem to take it in. 'That's really how he—!' My hand flew to my mouth. 'I knew something terrible had happened,' I whispered. 'Oh my God, supposing the guy had a knife or a gun?'

'He didn't luckily,' Lexie said, puffing out her cheeks.

'Just a rock-hard jaw,' Billie said with a grin.' Poor Oliver. That must have *really* hurt!'

'I'm going to find him!' I went flying off into the crowd looking for a sweet-faced boy with curly hair.

I tracked him down in the very grand functions room, where he was hopefully eyeing the vast wedding buffet, and made him tell me the whole story.

Oliver told me he had just gone out of the front door to go to school, when Eva's ex, who had obviously been lying in wait, came rushing up the path and tried to barge past Oliver, shouting for Eva to come and talk to him. Oliver told him very calmly and quietly that Eva didn't want to see him and he should just finally accept that and go away and cool down. Eva's ex made a second, even more desperate attempt to get past Oliver and that's when Oliver punched him on the jaw.

'Knocked him out cold,' he said with satisfaction, then gave me a sheepish grin. 'Just as well. I don't know what I'd have done if he punched me back! Eva's ex-boyfriend is a bit of a thug!'

'Oh, Oliver!' I gasped. 'You could have been really hurt!'

'I *was* really hurt!' he pointed out.

Oliver had spent the next few hours at A&E having his hand X-rayed and put in plaster, then he had to go down to the police station to give a statement. The boyfriend was arrested and was now up on a charge.

'Good!' I said heartlessly. 'Just a shame the police didn't believe you the first time.'

'My mum's totally disgusted,' he sighed.

'With the police?'

'With me! She says I'm no better than a hoodie, settling arguments with my fists.'

'You were defending Eva and your little sister,' I said angrily. 'What were you supposed to do? Suppose he'd got past you and really hurt somebody?'

He shrugged. 'To be fair to Mum, she had just got

back from Afghanistan! She was hoping to fall into bed to sleep off her jetlag. Instead she got a message telling her to come down to the local nick.' He rubbed his injured hand and gave me another sheepish grin. 'I tell you what, punching someone on the jaw hurts SO much worse in real life than it looks in the movies!'

'I think you were really brave,' I told him.

'I'm also really hungry,' he said plaintively.

I shook my head at him. 'Then get something to eat! There's enough food. You don't have to wait around being polite.'

'Actually it's more to do with only having one arm!' He gestured to his plaster cast.

'Oh my God, Oliver! I'm so *sorry*! I didn't think.' *Not for the first time, Natalie*, I thought.

I helped Oliver to a selection of titbits and we went to sit at a table to make it easier for him to eat. He was so hungry that for a while he munched in silence while I sat wondering when would be the right moment to tell him I was sorry.

'I–I bet I look a real freak in this dress,' I said awkwardly. 'Not to mention the hooker make-up.'

Oliver looked up from his plate. 'No, you look nice. A bit on the skinny side – but nothing that a few good meals wouldn't fix,' he added calmly.

I sighed. 'Wouldn't you know it?' I said, trying to joke. 'I finally find something I'm really good at and it's totally pointless.'

'You mean losing weight?'

I nodded, suddenly close to tears.

Oliver put down his fork. 'Not everything about it was pointless. You found out you like exercising. You learned you had willpower. You just need to know when to stop.'

'I've stopped,' I almost whispered, and realised it was true. 'I had two slices of toast for breakfast.'

'Excellent,' he said in the same reasonable voice as if he'd always known I'd eventually see sense.

I stole a glance at him. 'So – you don't think it was all just a stupid waste of time and energy?'

He thought for a minute. 'You could look at it like that,' he admitted with a sly grin. 'Or you could see it as a learning curve!'

'If you were a glass half-full kind of person,' I said, grinning, 'which luckily I am!'

I reached over and pinched one of Oliver's canapés and popped it in my mouth. 'I wish my mum could have been here to see Plum married,' I said wistfully. 'You know when Dad brought me back from that hideous school? He told me I was just like her. Nobody ever said that before.'

'Have you got a picture of her?' Oliver said unexpectedly.

I nodded. 'I've got two.'

'Can you still remember her face in the photo when you close your eyes?'

'I think so,' I said, puzzled.

'Then next time Jenny lays into you, telling you that you're clumsy or thick or whatever it is, just tune her out and picture your mum telling you that you're fine exactly the way you are. Which is true,' Oliver said, suddenly turning violent red. 'You are absolutely totally fine. Lovely, in fact.'

I couldn't speak. I was slightly struck dumb that a boy could say something so sweet.

'I should probably stop giving you unwanted advice,' he said, still flushing. 'I probably shouldn't have—'

'No, you should,' I said quickly. 'That's actually the best advice anyone ever—'

We would probably still be blushing at one another over Oliver's plate of canapés, but at that moment we were interrupted by Matilda, clutching at the front of her dress. 'Natalie, I really, *really* need a pee, and I can't find my mum and I can't—' she pulled anxiously at her dress.

'Don't worry, sweetie,' I told her. 'I'll take you there.' I swept her up and whizzed her through the wedding guests on the way to the nearest cloakroom.

In the foyer, I recognised some of our Norfolk neighbours, the Talbots, the people who let us keep our ponies at their stables. I hadn't realised Plum had invited them to the wedding. She must have told them they could bring some friends because Mr Talbot was talking loudly to a couple I didn't know.

I think Mr Talbot must have had a couple of drinks already. He certainly wasn't bothering to lower his voice. 'A real porker, she was as a teenager,' he bellowed at his friends so everybody could hear. 'Even her own brothers and sisters used to call her "Piggy"! But fair play to Jenny, she put herself on a diet and lost all that weight, then she set her cap at James Bonneville-St John and she hasn't looked back!'

'Why did you just stop for no reason?' Matilda asked, dismayed, as I stood paralysed in the middle of the foyer. 'I'm really bursting now, Natalie.'

'Almost there, sweetie,' I said automatically, though I was still reeling from what I'd heard.

To Matilda's and my relief we made it just in time. Afterwards I helped her rearrange her dress and wash her hands and we both had some of the gorgeous Jo

Malone hand cream in the dispensers.

On the way back we caught up with Nellie. 'I was thinking,' she said cheerfully, 'since we've both had so much fun at the gym, we should find a way to keep it up? You know, keep up the momentum?'

'I can't afford Jacek's gym,' I told her.

She laughed. 'Me neither! But we could go to zumba or yoga or pilates or something.' Then she said, 'Why are you looking at me like that? I'm serious. Plum and I have had a few heart-to-hearts recently and we agreed that we had to stop treating you like our pet project.'

'Can I have that in writing?' I said cautiously.

Nellie ruffled my hair. 'If you like!'

We'd found our way back the function room which was now heaving with people. I stood on tiptoe trying to locate Oliver in the crush. 'Are you looking for your friend with the bad hand?' Matilda said. 'Shall I find him for you?'

'That would be great,' I told her.

I turned back to my sister. 'So if I'm not your pet project, why are you trying to make me do zumba, whatever "zumba" is?'

'Oh my God, you'll love it. It's working out to Latin rhythms. It's so much fun!'

'You're very into fun suddenly. This wouldn't have

anything to do with Jacek, would it?' I said mischievously.

'*Ssh*!' Nellie hissed. 'She'll hear! She'll go mad because he's foreign and he doesn't practise law or work for a merchant bank.' 'She' meant my stepmother, who was standing just a few metres away.

'It's your life,' I said vaguely, but I was really thinking about a teenage girl whose own family taunted her by calling her 'Piggy'. No wonder Jenny was so obsessed with us being thin. No matter how much she dieted, my stepmother must still be haunted by that insecure overweight girl.

I saw her looking across at my dad, who had gone out into the foyer trying to make himself heard on his phone. I was about to go over to her and say something about how beautiful Plum looked in her wedding dress then I heard my stomach give a loud rumble as if it had only just noticed the buffet.

Without a second thought I grabbed a plate, piling it with enough food for me and Oliver. I eventually hunted him down in the gardens with Matilda, who was making him wear her flowery crown. I sat beside them on the grass and began to eat as though I hadn't eaten for months, which I actually hadn't.

When my friends come out with their plates of food

they saw me and Oliver contentedly sharing our favourite titbits and Lexie shrieked. 'Oh my God, Natalie! You have no idea how happy we are to see you stuffing your face like usual!'

'Me too,' I said through a mouthful of honeyed salmon.

It had been a kind of madness, but it was over. I could tell by the way I was shovelling in Plum's fabulous canapés three at a time feeling absolutely no guilt! My starved stomach was already bloating up like a beach ball and I would probably pay for it later, but I thought I could live with that.

We sat together under the willows, chatting and politely enduring Matilda's 'knock knock' jokes, as the sunshine glinted off the river, then Oliver said he had to leave. His mum was dropping him off for one of his rare visits to his dad. 'She thinks I need more fatherly input. She says she doesn't want me to end up joining a gang,' he said, rolling his eyes.

Billie choked on her canapé. 'Sorry, Oliver, but that is *funny*! The idea of you joining a gang!'

I went to wave him off then I ran back to the others, feeling my long dress pleasantly cool and swishy around my ankles. It dawned on me that I was ridiculously happy, happier than I'd been in years.

'Seeing as we missed today's Breakfast Club because of the wedding, and since everyone thinks I need fattening up, why don't we take Mario up on his offer and go after school and have pasta one night?' I suggested. 'My treat.'

'Oh, you are *on*!' Lexie gave me an enthusiastic thumbs up.

'Pasta followed by incredibly creamy ice-cream,' I added mischievously.

At that moment I looked up to see Jenny by herself on the hotel patio, holding her half-empty glass of champagne, and watching us as we laughed and hugged and made plans. I didn't think I could ever really love my stepmother, but for the first time, I felt a pang of real sympathy for her.

I am so much luckier than Jenny, I thought.

At least I had sisters who really cared about me, even if it had taken them a decade or so to figure that out! Then I turned to smile at Ella, Billie and Lexie, my crazy, funny, talented unofficial sisters.

And I've got you, I told them silently. *I've got the Breakfast Club.*

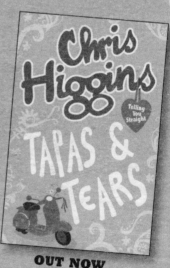

Chris Higgins

Telling You Straight

Eva wants to be the best at everything, just like her older sister, Amber. She's queen of the gym club and the girl everyone envies.

But when new girl Patty arrives in town, cracks begin to show in her perfect life and it's time for Eva to confront some hidden secrets …

OUT NOW

INTRODUCING
ELECTRA BROWN

Electra's family is falling apart. Her dad's moving out, her mum's given in to her daytime TV addiction and her little brother has just been caught shoplifting. Even the guinea pig's gone mental. Where can a girl turn in her hour of need?

'We love her!'
MIZZ

ALL BOOKS
OUT NOW!

Helen Bailey